The SCOT'S VOW

HIGHLAND HUNTERS 4

KEIRA MONTCLAIR

CHAPTER ONE

Autumn, The Borderlands of Scotland 1315

AFTER ALL THE times she'd hoped to prove her ability as an archer, Ceit MacAdam was about to have the best chance she'd ever had. A group of English reivers had raided a small village on Scottish land, holding the men hostage in an area in the middle of the huts, their tiny swords out of their sheaths. The wives and bairns of the men stood and watched, helpless to do much more than comfort each other while they watched the villains taunt the Scots. Ceit could have giggled at the size of the reivers' petite weapons, a far cry from the Scots' mighty swords.

Ceit was part of a patrol assigned by King Robert the Bruce to keep the English out of Scotland while the king himself was in Ireland assisting his brother. Their group was led by Maitland Menzie and Dyna Grant and was small enough to be nimble and stealthy but it was made up of the finest swordsmen and archers in Scotland. Ceit and her cousins Isla and Reyna, female archers all trained by their grandmother, the famed archer Gwyneth Ramsay, were a deadly force. This would be the first skirmish they'd had in a while.

Wee bairns cried and clung to their mother's skirts while the English bound up the few men of the village. At first Ceit couldn't understand why the Scots hadn't been able to overtake the small force, but then the truth reared its ugly head. Three of the Englishmen had separated three young lassies from their families. The filthy English held the girls pressed against them, running their dirty hands across the girls' breasts and faces in the most lewd manner. No one dared fight back lest the girls come to even greater harm.

"These are some fine lasses ye made. I plan to take all three," she heard one say, as he smiled while rubbing the girl's breast again, holding her close to his body while two creepy reivers held onto the others. "I like mine young, so I can feel their blood." His toothless grin made one girl scream and he slapped her. "Shut your mouth. Until I tell you to open it, you'll say nothing."

"I'd like her to open her mouth for me, Albert," the one next to him said, chuckling. Albert's hand swung out and slapped the back of the man's head. "Shut your mouth too. She's mine and only mine."

Then Albert licked the side of the girl's face while he placed both hands on her breasts, the poor lass cringing and sobbing.

That was a big mistake. Ceit turned to look

at their leaders, Maitland and Dyna, and she knew this would end quickly. Dyna yanked on her white braid, pulling it tight, a habit she had whenever her fury got the best of her. Ceit had seen her do it many times. Maitland hid his fury better. She could only catch the twitch in his jaw, and it was twitching now.

Maitland would make his move quicker with bairns and the young lasses involved. Usually, he took his time to make sure their timing was perfect. He wouldn't wait in this case, she could see it in the tense line of his jaw. They would definitely be attacking soon. Ceit wiped the sweat from her palms, never a good thing for an archer to have.

Maitland gave his brief instructions as to where each of the archers was to go and how the swordsmen would approach, giving the archers time to place themselves. Once they were ready, he let out the Menzie war whoop, signaling the battle was on.

Ceit had been told to lead her horse to a safe spot, then fire arrow after arrow until their mission was accomplished. King Robert had given their patrol simple instructions: Protect the border.

And they were about to do so.

As soon as Maitland let out his war whoop, Ceit sent her horse into a gallop to a copse where she could shoot safely, her blood now racing through her veins as she joined Isla and Reyna behind the oak trees. Reyna and Isla both climbed, but Ceit stayed on her horse and began firing. She missed with her first arrow, but she made an instant adjustment and her second and third landed true, hitting two different Englishmen.

Shouts of fear and pain bellowed from the line of the skirmish, mostly from the Englishmen daring to come toward them. Others hid, but she could see them well. Wulf and Griff rode next to Maitland while Dyna joined Ysenda and Thea on the opposite side of the path, where the bushes and trees gave great cover.

Wulf struck two men off their horses, then bellowed, "Reyna, be careful. There are archers on one of the cottages."

Reyna shouted, "I'm fine! Fight and dinnae worry about me!"

Then Ceit noticed an Englishman running with a torch headed straight for a hut, surely meaning to start the thatched roof on fire. "Fire!" Isla yelled.

All three of them nocked an arrow and aimed at the man. One struck his hand, one hit his flank, the other in the arse.

Ceit couldn't help but wonder which arrow was hers.

"Nice work, lasses," Maitland bellowed. Another tried to do the same thing, using a torch to start the roof on fire. "Another!"

"We'll get him," Ceit hollered.

The three shot again, one arrow missing and the other two finding their mark. Ceit shot another arrow and caught him in the leg this time.

She'd been aiming for his belly. Dammit!

The Scots patrol continued until there were

only a dozen Englishmen left. Ceit knew that though the English fought hard, the skirmish would be over if only the village men hadn't been tied up. She weighed her choices, searching for a way to release the men without being seen. There were about ten homes with a few small buildings for animals. The men were kept in a makeshift courtyard, a place where the villagers had often gathered around a pit for roasting meat. The main water well sat not far away, various buckets on the ground nearby.

The women and children had rushed back inside the buildings as soon as the arrows started to fly, though most of them had gone into the same two huts. The English had let the lasses go in order to fight, and they had also run for safety inside a cottage.

It was cool, but not overly cold, something she appreciated because her hands stayed nimble in warmer weather. Firing arrows in the winter didn't work well for her. After her gaze caught the eyes of some of the women inside the huts, the worry on their faces went straight to her heart, their youngest bairns clutched tightly against them. She had to help these people.

She dismounted from her horse, creeping toward the Scots through the driest area she could find, using the cottages, pens, and troughs to hide between. Creeping behind a tree closest to one of the men, she decided it was worth a try in order to even their numbers. If the English stayed strong, one of her patrol mates could be hurt. That couldn't happen. She pulled her dagger out, hoping to cut the men free so they could use their swords and help with the battle.

She crept toward the men, one step at a time, holding her breath. Sounds of battle carried over the area, the clash of metal, screams of pains, grunts of men who hefted weapons high. Her bow hung haphazardly over her shoulder, knocking into her quiver but not loud enough to be heard amidst the screams and yells. Having reached the area behind the fighting Englishmen, she had to make sure she wasn't in the firing line of her own archers.

One of the Scots saw her and said, "Hurry, lass." He held his arms out at the best angle so she could cut the ropes quickly. She freed this man and was about to free the next one when the enemy changed their stance.

Some of the English must have heard the Scotsman's call and now five of her enemy spun about to face her. She dropped her dagger and nocked an arrow, taking out the first one who'd aimed at her. Another went down with an arrow in his back, fired from the trees where her cousins still perched. Maitland took the third one down with his sword while Ceit aimed for the fourth man.

The fifth man had disappeared from her sight and was nearly on top of her before she saw him coming from her left side with his sword drawn, but Dyna fired and caught him in the chest just as his sword swung down in an arc aimed straight for her arm. She ducked the major hit and the arrow took the power out of him, but not before his blade caught the edge of her thigh.

The English were now all down, fortunately.

Dyna yelled, "How did ye no' see him, Ceit? He'd have killed ye for certes."

The others joined her, concern etched over their faces while Dobbin cut the rest of the Scots free and the others came out of the cottage.

"I dinnae know. I was focused on the ones in front of me. I only focus on one at a time so I can be accurate." The truth of the situation was finally hitting her, the blood running down her leg, a slow burn building. She had the oddest feeling she was looking at someone else's leg.

"Ye did a fine job on two of them while Reyna hit one and Maitland got the other, but this one could have finished ye." Dyna shook her head as she headed toward her, but then stopped, staring at her leg. "Ye need stitching."

Ceit peered at her leg as if she were in another world. Multiple voices echoed in her ear, but the sharp pain from the large laceration finally had her attention more than anything else. She was bleeding a fine river of red. Someone took her by the elbow and said, "I'll fix it." It wasn't a voice she knew, but a woman from the cottage.

Reyna and Dyna went with her. Dyna said, "She'll stop the bleeding and put a linen bandage on it. Tie it tightly, please."

The Scottish woman nodded and said, "I'll fix her up nicely, give her something for the pain. We owe you for saving us all."

Dyna said, "Nay, no pain potions. We have to get her to Ramsay land."

"Back again?" Reyna asked.

"Aye, think ye that ye are the only one of Logan's granddaughters we must be careful with?" drawled Dyna. "We take her back to Ramsay land because we are the closest. Besides, our king often sends messages to Logan if we are out on patrol. I dinnae know where we are to go next. This was a random group of reivers in the Borderlands. I dinnae wish to go all the way into England, so back we go. Aunt Brenna can stitch her if this kind woman can get the bleeding slowed."

The woman took Ceit inside a clean cottage, giving orders to two daughters she had inside. "Clean water and linen strips to go around her leg. And one square piece first." The daughters hurried, handing her the square piece which she placed against Ceit's thigh and put pressure on it. Ceit did her best not to groan whenever the woman increased her pressure on the wound.

"How bad is it?" Reyna asked, Isla joining them.

Isla looked at it and said, "Not verra deep, but enough that Grandmama will wish to stitch it up."

"Shall I stitch now?" the kind woman asked. "I have a needle."

"Nay, my grandmother is Brenna Ramsay. She'll insist on cleaning it first," Isla explained. "Stop the bleeding, then wrap her tight and we'll get her home before the end of the day."

The others went back outside, leaving Ceit with the village woman. "Many thanks for helping me," Ceit said to the red-haired woman. She couldn't have been more than five years older than Ceit was herself, yet she had two daughters already.

"Nay, we owe you for saving us." Her kind eyes locked on hers. "I hate to think about what those men would have done to my daughters." She glanced over them as her eyes teared up briefly. "Brenna Ramsay is yer grandmama? Ye are a fortunate one."

"Nay, she's my aunt and she's a wonderful healer."

"Tell me something. I heard she insists on everything being clean. Why? I think it would be more important to get things done quickly, in a hurry. We dinnae wash our hands all the time, yet I hear she insists on it. We have sons that have worked for Ramsay guards in the past, and they always tell them to wash. I think 'tis wasteful of the water."

Ceit thought for a moment. "Ye are correct that she is fastidious about cleanliness when it comes to her tools and her hands, but I think 'tis just her way. Some people have clean homes like ye do, and some don't. She wishes to be a clean healer. Other than that, I dinnae know."

She made a mental note to ask her dear aunt because the woman made sense. Growing up on Ramsay land, they always had to be clean about themselves, yet as bairns, they often argued about it.

The woman finished her work and bound her

leg. She got down from the table she sat on, if a wee bit too quickly, then stifled a groan. It was surely going to be a painful ride home.

Maitland entered and wrapped one arm around her shoulders. "Lean on me, Ceit. I'll get ye to yer horse. We're leaving right away. The men here said they would bury the English. We can go home, and I'd prefer to hurry with yer injury."

"'Tis no' so bad, Maitland. I may no' need to go home."

"Oh, we are going back to Ramsay land, not just because of yer injury but because there is another message awaiting us. Before we leave, I must ask ye a question."

"Go ahead." Her heartbeat sped up because she feared he was going to ask her the one question she did not wish to hear.

"How the hell did ye no' see that man coming up on ye?"

And there it was. Her one fear. Tearing apart how she acted in a skirmish, that she'd made a mistake and been caught, but he'd also focused on the one thing that worried her more than any other. Her sight.

Dammit.

CHAPTER TWO

BRIN CAMERON HEADED into the keep after a short patrol of Cameron land, not finding anything of interest. He'd finished his duties training their guards, something he did often because their job was to protect both Cameron land and Lochluin Abbey. But his heart wasn't in it at the moment. The only thing he had on his mind was a big, fat lamb meat pie. A tasty hunk of crusty bread would go nicely with an ale.

The sun had just dropped so it was time to end his day and relax a bit. As soon as he opened the door to the keep, he noticed his parents seated next to the hearth. The serving lasses were busy cleaning up the debris from the evening's meal. He waved to one lass, and she hurried back toward the kitchen to grab a platter for him.

They were used to seeing him come in late. He didn't like eating with the usual crowd from the small village nearby and the guards. There were always too many questions about his lack of a wife.

And too many lasses offering themselves.

"Brin, I'm glad to see ye. Come sit with us for a moment." His mother, the former Jennie Grant, waved him over and he complied. How he missed having his sisters Tara and Riley around so their attention was on someone other than him.

His father, Aedan Cameron, the chieftain of Clan Cameron, moved a chair so Brin took the indicated chair between the two. His mother reached over and brushed some stray hairs away from his face. "My, but ye have grown into such a handsome man, Brin."

He said nothing and let his mother do what she wished, but mostly because they were the only ones in the great hall. "My thanks, Mama." He adored both his parents so he hated to disappoint them.

His sire said, "Jennie, he's a grown man. Take yer hands away."

His mother mumbled, "Forgive me." She smiled and looked at her husband. "Aedan and I have been discussing the subject ye dislike most—yer lack of a wife. I know ye dinnae like us prying, but yer father thinks we must."

He let out a big sigh, unwilling to let them think he'd already found someone he was interested in. But he had recently met a woman from Clan Ramsay, one of their finest allies, who he wished to pursue. Ceit MacAdam had stirred something in him that he hadn't felt in many years.

Ceit was on patrol for their king at present, so it would be difficult to initiate a relationship. But her green eyes hadn't left his mind since the patrol had stopped on Cameron land not long ago. He had enjoyed talking with her, found her mind curious and wise, and she was a highly skilled archer, as most Ramsay females were. But he would not share any of his thoughts about Ceit with his parents. He needed to know her better first.

"Brin, I know ye wish for us to stay around forever, but we canno'. And old age seems to be creeping up on me. Ye need to find a wife if ye wish to be chieftain someday."

"Da, ye know I dinnae need a wife to be chieftain." Brin couldn't help but glare into the blue eyes that mirrored his own. He looked more like his sire than his mother.

His mother said, "But yer sire says ye must. We dinnae wish to lose everything we have worked so hard to maintain. And yer forefathers. If ye never marry, ye will never have a legitimate son. Ye must have an heir."

"Riley or Tara's lads could become chieftains. What about Tevis? He's a fine lad. He could be chieftain someday."

"'Tis no' the same," his sire grumbled. "His name is Massie and he's my grandson, not my son. Tevis Massie. He grew up on Black Isle."

His mother's tone dropped to a low voice. "Brin, ye canno' allow one lass to color yer view of all lasses."

And why not? That's what he'd like to ask. How did he know they weren't all the same?

"Ye were young," his mother persisted, as if she'd read his thoughts.

"I was, but it doesnae change the result of it."

Brin was not going to go through this again with his parents. The same words had been said multiple times.

Nearly five and ten years ago, he'd fallen in love. Hard. Abigall MacKie had been his first love, and the first woman he'd ever had relations with. Now when he looked back on that love he thought he had, he was forced to consider that others had been right at the time.

It hadn't been true love, but lust.

But then Abigall had broken his heart and stomped on it.

And ever since that moment when she'd looked at him and told him she'd chosen another, he swore he'd never fall in love again. Oh, there had been other women over the fifteen years, but none had ever grabbed a piece of his heart like Abigall had.

"Brin, will ye think on it, please? I know ye have dated others, but none that have ever been serious. Ye need to have someone in yer life, have wee bairns about ye. There must be someone ye could be interested in, someone ye could share yer life with. I hate to see ye alone."

"I promise I will, Mama." He rose from the chair and took his ale with him, needing to end the conversation before he slipped. Giving in and sharing his interest in the lass would mark her, meaning that whenever she came to Cameron land, they'd be right there to talk with her. He couldn't handle that. If he was to find out more about her, it had to be without the supervision of his parents. He was in his fourth decade of his life, after all.

So he walked away because he couldn't bear to hurt his parents anymore. But even with that consideration, there was not a chance he would mention Ceit's name. He couldn't deal with his mother's excitement if he chose someone she already knew—especially a Ramsay.

Ceit hated to admit how pleased she was to finally come upon Ramsay land. She agreed with Maitland and Dyna's assessment. She needed to go home to her dear Aunt Brenna, the best healer in the world. Her aunt would talk softly the way she always did, settle her insides with just one look and her soothing voice. The woman was amazing and was the only one she wanted stitching her wound, though she bet Aunt Brenna's sister, Jennie Cameron, would be much the same.

She nearly fell off her horse when the shot of pain struck her, but she hung on, Dyna coming up on one side of her. "We're nearly there. Ye can make it."

"I will," she said, fighting to keep her eyes open. She was exhausted and in pain. Would she be able to sleep?

"Once Aunt Brenna gives ye the first dose of the potion, ye willnae feel the stitches so much. And after the second dose, ye'll be sound asleep. 'Tis by far the best way to heal."

As they approached the gates, she recognized a few faces on horseback, here to escort the group to the stables. The chieftain, her cousin Torrian, hollered out, "Everyone is hale? Anyone need a healer?"

Maitland pointed to Ceit. "Just one. Minor wound, but she needs stitches."

Her grandfather called out from his horse, "Good thing ye brought her back."

Dyna glanced over at Ceit with a smug smile, "I knew we had to bring ye home. I dinnae care to have a target on my back from Uncle Logan."

Ceit rolled her eyes, then moved through the gate and headed to the stables, her horse as happy to be here as she was. "I'm fine, Grandda." She could feel the man's astute gaze on her.

"What happened?" her mother called out as soon as she saw Ceit on her horse near the stables.

"Naught that matters much, Mama. I'm fine." She supposed the blood on her leggings or the bandage on her leg made it appear otherwise.

"Doesnae look like ye are fine. Cailean!" She let out a roar and Ceit's father came running.

"What is...? Never mind. I'll carry her, Sorcha. I can see why ye called for me." The look on her poor father's face nearly broke her heart. His hair was braided on the sides, like he often wore it, just like Maitland's. It kept his hair from looking as if it were a total mess. It was two shades darker than her mother's golden waves, much like her own, but his green eyes looked exactly like hers. Having two parents with green eyes made her own seem even richer, or so she thought.

"Papa, I'm fine. 'Tis just a wee scratch," she

pleaded. "I can walk on my own." She dismounted and winced moments before her sire scooped her up into his strong arms.

"'Tis no scratch. Scratches dinnae leave yer leggings drenched with blood."

"Papa…" she moaned.

"Cease yer arguing, lass. I'll carry ye to yer Aunt Brenna's." The expression on her father's face told her there would be no arguing about it.

Her grandsire came barreling down the path behind her, her grandmother approaching from the keep. "Sounds like yer sire has the right of it, Ceit MacAdam. I've seen wounds like that, and they are far from scratches."

She scowled at her grandfather who narrowed his gaze at her. "Dinnae frown at me, lass," he warned.

"Logan, would ye consider that she might be in some pain?" her grandmother chided. "Leave the wounded lass alone."

Her father added, "I have her, Logan. I think Gwyneth gave the best advice. We'll both have our say but not until after she sees Aunt Brenna."

Her mother followed her father with their unified attack on her grandsire. "Papa, stay back, if ye please. Ye make everyone unsettled when ye start bellowing."

"Sorcha, I'll do as I wish!"

"Not with my daughter, ye'll no'! Exactly as I said. Stop yelling," her mother said, stopping to place her hands on her curvaceous hips. "Leave her be for now. Ye'll have yer say later."

Ceit nearly laughed when she caught the curve of her father's lips. She whispered, "I saw that, Papa."

"I love it when yer mother yells at her father. I admit it. She's one of the few who dares to give it back to him." He did his best to whisper, but his voice was too deep.

"I heard that, MacAdam."

"If ye'd stay back as ye were instructed, ye would no' have heard aught."

Maitland ran ahead of the group arguing and held the door open to the keep for her sire. He whispered, "I'll keep him back, Ceit." Then he spun around and approached her grandsire. "Uncle Logan, I have a question for ye when ye have the time. 'Tis about the battle we just experienced."

"If ye need my help, of course."

"Many thanks from all of us, Maitland," her grandmother called out as she closed the door to the keep behind her, leaving the two outside.

Aunt Brenna already stood in the doorway to the healing chamber, waiting for them.

"Tell me what happened, Ceit."

"A sword to my thigh. We stopped the bleeding," she explained as her father set her down on the table her aunt used most. Then he set a stool under her foot so she could extend her leg out far enough for her aunt to have a good look.

Aunt Brenna unwrapped the binding, tossing the bloodied fabric into a bin behind her. "Hmmm. It looks like a clean cut, but I think it still needs to be stitched."

Cailean paled and looked at her mother. "Ye are in charge now."

He left as fast as he could and her aunt whispered, "Was that fast enough for ye, Sorcha?"

Ceit glanced at her mother, oddly curious about the interchange. "What?"

"Yer sire nearly passes out if he sees anything to do with blood and his bairns. For me too. He canno' handle it so Auntie sent him away before he could drop to the ground."

"Every time," Aunt Brenna declared with a smile. "Finally, he accepts it."

Her grandmother entered next. "Did I hear ye mention blood and stitching, Brenna?" She wore the same grin Aunt Brenna did. "I see Cailean running outside. We all know what that means, especially when he turns that fine shade of green."

"Works like a charm with that man. I will stitch, but first I must clean it."

Ceit watched her dear aunt's skilled hands as she gathered her tools, being careful to keep everything clean. Thinking on the words of the woman who'd helped her near the Borderlands, she asked, "Why do ye keep everything so clean, Aunt Brenna? 'Tis no' like there are any bugs walking on the surfaces."

"'Twas my mother's way. She and her father tested it because she thought it to be so, but Grandda didnae believe her. But they found the wounds that were cleaned carefully healed faster than the dirty wounds. And they tested using clean hands too. They stayed with it and so have

Jennie and I. We believe it works better. Why do ye ask?"

"Because the woman who helped bind my wound doesn't believe in it, but she'd heard about yer beliefs."

The door burst open and two strode in—Isla and Thea. "She will heal, Grandmama?" Thea asked.

"Aye, she'll be fine."

"Good," said Isla, taking a seat across from her. "May I ask her a question, Grandmama?"

Ceit said, "Of course. I'm fine."

"You missed," Isla stated. "What happened?"

Ceit blushed, though she was not surprised. Her vision had dimmed on her once when she was fighting. "Nay, I found my mark."

"Aye, but ye were always better than that. Ye hit the first in the arse. Reyna and I stopped him. Then yer next arrow missed completely."

"But no' the next one," she argued, hating that her grandmother was listening. She hoped she hadn't been paying attention.

Apparently her grandmother had, because her hands fisted on her thin hips before she yelled at the two. "Get out. Both of ye."

"What?" Isla asked, looking at her grandmother for help. "But Aunt Gwyneth canno' send me out. Grandmama, 'tis yer healing chamber and I wish to stay."

Aunt Brenna stopped to stare at her granddaughter, pointing her finger at Isla. "Dinnae look at me with such judgment. Isla, ye remind me of yer mother so much that it scares me, but listen to me. Ye are wrong to accuse someone who is about to be stitched, especially with a large gaping wound on the top of her leg. Ye think that doesnae hurt her? Go away. Save yer questions for later. Even yer mother knows better."

Isla crossed her arms with a scowl, but Thea said, "My apologies, Ceit. Fare thee well. Leave her be, Isla. Grandmama is right. My mother would be verra upset with us." Thea's mother, Bethia, was Brenna's eldest daughter.

The two departed, but it only took a moment for her grandmother to turn back around to her and ask, "So is it that ye can no longer shoot or is it yer eyes?"

"What do ye mean?" Ceit asked, hating being drawn into this conversation.

"Are ye going blind like me?"

CHAPTER THREE

——~~——

BRIN STEPPED INTO the courtyard after a
long ride the next day. His training of the
men had taken up most of his morning so he'd
saved his ride until after the midday meal. He
needed it to think. He had much thinking to
do, especially when it came to his parents. They
would not force a wedding on him. It wasn't
their choice, and he feared they would cross that
line and start telling him who to marry.

He had to be alone to think on what he would
do next. Staying here until his parents found him
another lass to betroth him to was not the best
prospect for him. He wished to disappear for a
wee bit, but that was unlikely to happen.

He came through the gates and groaned, having
forgotten that his parents had planned a small
festival for the villagers.

And who did his eyes fall upon as soon as he
took two steps into the middle of the festivities?
None other than Abigall Dunnet, now married
to the MacVie chieftain, Odgar. Clan MacVie
was an hour away but they usually showed up

whenever free food was handed out. MacVie had a large appetite.

The love of his life stood a short distance away from him and he would surely have to speak with her. Blast it all to hell and back. It was nearly five and ten years later and Abigall MacVie still looked as lovely as ever, even with her protruding belly. Her husband Odgar stood next to her, his own belly nearly as big as Abigall's, but it didn't seem to affect him one bit. "Greetings, Cameron. Still unmarried, I see. Mayhap there is no one for ye." Then he gave him a crooked grin, waggling his brow at him. "Or do ye like the animals in the stable better?"

"My choice, MacVie. Glad to see ye are well, Abigall." He nodded to her, his gaze locking on her brown eyes. He swore there was a sadness there he'd never seen before.

"Her name is Lady MacVie to ye, Cameron." His dark curly hair had turned into a frizz that looked as though it hadn't been washed or tended in days. Completely different from Abigall's light brown hair that had nary a strand out of place. What had she seen in him?

"Odgar, he can call me Abigall." Her voice wasn't as confident as it used to be.

"I said nay," he grabbed her elbow and pinched, as if warning her to agree.

"Take yer hands from her," Brin advised.

Odgar snorted. "Ye canno' tell me what to do with my wife. I'll do as I please. As ye can see, I have proven my superiority since this will be our third bairn."

Brin stepped forward until he was nearly touching Odgar—nose to nose. "On my land, ye will do as I say or get off." He was pleased to learn that he was a half hand taller than Odger. Looking down at him pleased him. Why had he thought the man was a hand taller than he was several years ago?

"'Tis yer sire's land, no' yers," Odgar barked back. "I hear ye are afraid of taking on the laird's duties." The two stood toe-to-toe, neither moving.

"Hurt her again and ye'll feel my fist, and then I'll drag ye from Cameron land myself from the back of my horse. Matters no' who the laird is. Still my land. Care to see how many supporters ye have here?"

Odgar stepped back, paling just enough to please Brin. Abigall's voice interrupted them. "Please, I'd like to find something to eat, Odgar." Abigall couldn't hide her blush over her husband's rudeness. "The bairn is hungry."

Brin said, "We have a table full of meat pies inside, Abigall. And some fruit tarts too. Please help yerself." Then he glared at Odgar and stepped away, heading toward the great hall for a meat pie of his own.

He strode quickly inside, surprised to hear a familiar loud bark of his name from the area near the hearth. "About time ye got here, Cameron!"

Padraig Grant stood next to Brin's mother, his wife Giselle seated in a chair and covered in a warm blanket.

"Padraig! Pleased to see ye. What brings ye to

Cameron land?" Seeing his dear cousin pleased him, especially since he rarely saw him after he married Giselle Matheson. Before, Padraig had trained with Brin's Uncle Ruari, and he'd spent a great deal of time on Cameron land. They'd become good friends because of it.

Brin rushed over, forgetting about Abigall and how badly it still hurt to see her with anyone but him.

Padraig drawled, "My wife thinks she's about to have our bairn and decided she wished to have a healer present instead of having me assist her. Can ye believe it?"

How Brin loved his cousin Padraig's tendency for sarcasm and jesting. He had a way of lighting up the entire room with his wit and laughter. If he'd had a mouthful of ale, he'd have spewed it out when he looked at Giselle, her hand rubbing her well-rounded belly with pursed lips. "I dinnae know, Brin. Would ye wish to have Padraig responsible for yer bairn? I prefer Aunt Jennie." She rolled her eyes at him, shaking her head at the same time. "Take him away, please, Brin. I canno' stand it any longer. He's making me daft."

Brin grabbed a meat pie and said, "Grab a couple, Padraig. I've been charged with granting yer wife a wee bit of peace." He leaned over to kiss Giselle's cheek. "Ye look wonderful, Giselle. Mama will take fine care of ye." Then he stood and kissed his mother's cheek before leading Padraig away.

He led the way, but Padraig put a show on for all the villagers seated at the trestle tables, walking backward toward the keep door. "I'll miss ye, my love." Then he feigned tripping and yelled, "See, I'm falling for yer heart all over again."

Giselle waved at him, with quite a dismissive angle to the movement, sending others into giggles.

Padraig's hands covered his heart. "I love ye so much, Giselle. Ye are the love of my life. Forever and ever."

"I love ye too, husband. Go now." She rolled her eyes for emphasis.

"I'll return soon, as ye know I canno' stand to be apart from ye for long…"

"Padraig!" Giselle shouted. "Just go!"

Brin grabbed the back of his collar and yanked him out the door, slamming it behind them. "Leave the poor lass alone. My mother always tells me how difficult the last moon of carrying a bairn is for a lass. Says 'tis like having a sack of dirt tied to yer belly and getting in the way of everything."

Padraig laughed and shrugged. "My bairn may look like a bag of dirt too. I'm just trying to keep poor Giselle smiling. She is having a difficult time riding a horse. She wished to get back to Matheson land to have her bairn, but we may no' make it."

"Truly?"

"Aye, the healer in Edinburgh said she had less than a moon, and she had to get moving. I dinnae know if we will make it or no', but she said Aunt Jennie was the next best thing, so here we are. She may still make me leave, but I hope yer mother convinces her to stay here."

"A new bairn would be nice," Brin said. Padraig hadn't changed much over the years, his brown hair hanging in waves to his collar. If anything, he looked a wee bit more distinguished, a word that didn't fit the man, but he guessed it was probably the result of aging and the thoughts of his impending fatherhood.

"Now or never! After all these years, neither of us could believe she was truly carrying."

"Yer first?"

"Aye, we've tried many times over the years, but it never came to be. Caring for sick bairns has eased the pain. But enough about us. Tell me about that bastard Odgar."

"Ye know of him?"

"Aye, I know the look of hate I see from yer eyes, Brin Cameron. And ye dinnae send that hate to many. Was that the lass ye loved so long ago?"

Brin sighed, a bit too loudly apparently because Padraig arched a brow. "That obvious? Aye, I did fall for her. I fell in love, but she loved Odgar. Rejected my proposal."

Padraig snorted. "I think I can have some fun with that one, or do ye no' see it?"

They made their way to the stable, each saddling and mounting their horse, heading out through the gates. Brin motioned for Padraig to watch his tongue until they were alone again. Once they were clear in the meadow, Brin slowed his mount. "Fun? How can ye have fun with that fool?"

"I'm free to speak now?" Padraig glanced quickly over both shoulders before grinning at Brin with his usual odd look of glee. "Please allow me the chance to entertain ye, Brin. Ye look in need of it."

Brin chuckled because he knew Padraig so well. "Go ahead. Get it out of yer innards. Let yer thoughts spew freely."

Padraig chuckled then declared, "Odgar has the face of an old goat compared to ye, Brin."

Brin knew he would continue, that he should stop him, but he decided Padraig needed a few more laughs. And so did Brin.

"If Giselle has a wee lassie, she'll have bigger muscles than Odgar. He looks like he pinches boils on his cattle for entertainment."

Brin chuckled at that one.

"Abigall goes to sleep every night dreaming of ye rather than look at that face of his...what did Loki used to say?" He thought for a moment, scratching his beard. "Looking at that surly pignut!"

Brin laughed. "Enough. I'll fall off my horse if ye dinnae stop."

"I'll stop, but now I'll ask ye something serious," Padraig stated.

"Go ahead, everyone else does." He knew what was coming. Why hadn't he married yet?

"How could ye allow one lass to tie yer insides up so? She's lost to ye, so get over her and find another. There's a lovely lass out there for ye somewhere." Padraig stopped his horse and faced him. "Move on."

"Ye sound the same as my parents. They've said those exact words many times over the years. I'll marry someone, but…" He didn't know if he could admit the truth of it all.

"But?"

"But I'll probably never love her because I dinnae want my heart broken again. I'll choose someone, get married to make everyone happy, and become the chieftain of this nice small clan before my sire passes on. 'Tis what everyone wishes."

Padraig arched his brow. "And what do ye want, Brin?"

He stared at Padraig, shocked. He'd never been asked that question before. And he wasn't exactly sure how he wished to answer it. Or perhaps he did. "What do I want?" He paused again. "Some excitement. To be in battle somewhere with a beautiful archer and get lost in the excitement of strategizing against the English bastards who are always trying to ruin the Scots."

"Any archer in particular?"

"Nay, just… just someone different."

"Then I have the perfect answer for ye. Go on patrol. There are several out with the English trying to take over all our castles. I'm sure ye know of Maitland Menzie's group with Dyna Grant, but there are others out there as well. King Robert doesnae wish to lose any ground while he's assisting his brother."

Brin nearly snorted. "My sire would never allow it. My mother would have an attack of fainting if

I left. They are barely surviving losing Riley and Tara to Clan Matheson."

"But they have survived. And ye were no' meant to spend yer entire life pleasing yer parents. Ye must find yer purpose. Clearly, ye havenae."

"My purpose?" What the hell was Padraig talking about? "What does that mean? What is yer purpose?"

"My purpose is two-fold: taking care of sick bairns and loving Giselle. What is yers?"

Brin frowned. "How the hell would I know my purpose?"

He had no idea.

CHAPTER FOUR

CEIT SAT IN her mother's chamber, her leg propped up to keep the pain at bay. "Walking makes it worse. I canno' wait until it heals so it doesnae pull every time I move."

Her mother was busy making another outfit for Gavin's wee son. Her nimble fingers never stopped when she said, "Time will heal yer wound. The question is what do ye plan to do next? The patrol is leaving in two days. Da said Maitland was told to head north. There are problems near Inverness and King Robert wishes for yer group to assist in sending the English south again. How did they get that far north?"

Ceit sat up, instantly reinvigorated. "North? We're going north?"

Her grandmother came in just as her mother made that statement, taking a chair near the hearth before she picked up a blanket that needed repairing. "So Logan says. Maitland said they were ready to go. Dyna said in two days they'll be leaving."

"Good! I'm ready to move on." Ceit straightened

in her chair, the thought of patrolling again better than sitting in this chamber all day.

Both her mother and grandmother stopped what they were doing to stare at her. "Ye think ye can ride a horse with yer leg like that?"

She had to scowl over that thought. Dammit it all to hell, it would hurt. "Mayhap no' this day, but I'll be fine soon enough."

Both continued to stare at her. Ceit didn't know what to say so she stared back. "What?"

Her grandmother sighed and set the torn blanket down. "Sorcha, 'tis time to have my chat with the lass."

"Go ahead, Mama." Her mother tossed her long golden waves over her shoulder, her green eyes sparkling with some thought Ceit didn't wish to hear. Clearly, they'd conferred on this issue already and she didn't like it.

Ceit frowned, wondering why the two had discussed her situation. She decided to wait rather than start the argument at this point. She was going on that patrol whether they wanted her to or not.

Her grandmother folded her hands in her lap and asked, "How is yer sight?"

That was the one question she didn't wish to hear, a question that took her by surprise. "'Tis fine. Why do ye ask?"

"Others thought yer sight might be failing ye. What do ye think?" Grandmama asked, leaning forward, her clever eyes taking everything in about Ceit.

She hated when Grandmama did that—studied

you like you were a new villain about to steal one of her bairns away.

"I think my sight is fine." She lifted her chin a notch, hoping that would end the discussion.

"Reyna thought you missed with one shot. Something I didnae expect to hear about ye. Ceit, ye are one of the strongest archers I've trained."

Now she was just plain annoyed. Everyone knew that grandsire thought Reyna was the best archer now, so why would she be critical of others? She'd have to find a time to chat with her dear cousin. "Mayhap I get nervous in true battle. Has Reyna ever thought of that? Or Isla? They have men watching over them. Wulf hardly ever pulls his gaze from Reyna, and Grif does the same with Isla. I have no one. I get nervous. 'Tis all there is to it."

Her grandmother cast a glance over at her mother who pursed her lips but said naught. Then Grandmama narrowed her gaze at her. "Ye know that Grandpapa thinks ye and Reyna are both extremely talented. He doesnae favor one over the other. Ye are both his granddaughters and he adores ye both equally."

She snorted. "I think we all know who his favorite is."

Her mother said, "Lainey is the youngest. 'Tis the only reason he focuses on her. He did the same with ye for many years. But that is no' the issue we need to focus on."

"Then what is?" Ceit asked. She couldn't really argue about Lainey because the lass was overly cute in her leggings, tunic, and her wee bow.

Her mother's voice came out in that soft tone that told her how serious she was with her words. "Ceit, if there is anything wrong with yer sight, 'tis no' a reason to panic. Grandmama's eyesight has diminished over the years, so ye could be just like her. There are others who lose the keenness in their sight as they grow older. 'Tis no' unusual, so please dinnae panic."

"I'm no' old, and what if I lose my sight completely? What if I go blind? I've heard of others who have had it happen. The guards are always teasing me about some guard who canno' see his sword in front of him." Now she was rambling on and she knew she needed to stop, but the conversation was not going the way she wished it to go. In fact, now she was so upset over the conversation, she bolted off the bed with a yelp and awkwardly left the chamber. She nearly closed the door, but then stopped, turned back and whispered, "I can see just fine."

Ceit could not discuss the possibility of losing her sight any longer.

Once inside the passageway, she closed the door and waited. Sure enough, her mother said, "There must be some way we can test her to see if she is losing her sight."

"For what purpose?" Grandmama asked. "I've asked Brenna many times. There is naught to be done about it so why frighten the lass any more than she already is? She gave ye a solid answer, Sorcha. I recall being so upset when I was fighting that I could no' shoot a straight arrow no matter what. Yer sire will speak to it."

"I know, Mama. Duff. Ye panicked."

"But I did get him, the bastard."

Ceit turned away at that thought because she'd nearly forgotten that story. Her grandmother had tried to kill the man who killed her sire, but she'd missed over and over. Only her grandsire had been able to help her get past her nervousness.

That was it.

She wasn't losing her sight. She was just unsettled.

And she'd not think on it again. She limped her way down the passageway and the stairs, just noticing that there appeared to be a meeting taking place in the great hall, one led by Dyna and Maitland.

"Come join us, Ceit," Dyna yelled, stopping the conversation they were having. "We are making adjustments ye need to be aware of, and we need to learn yer intentions."

Ceit did her best to cover her injury, but she was unable to hide the hobbling it took to keep from ripping her stitches.

"Ye look better, cousin," Reyna said with a wide smile. Wulf sat beside her, his arm around her shoulders.

The two were always touching. And Reyna was happier than Ceit had ever seen her. As was Isla. Perhaps Ceit was just a wee bit jealous. She'd never had any relationship with a man.

"My thanks to ye," Ceit said, taking a seat on the bench. Maitland grabbed a stool and set it in front of her so she could prop her leg up to keep from bending it. "I hear we are headed north. I'm sure I'll be well enough to leave in a couple of days."

Dyna said, "Ye are no' leaving in a couple of days. I'll stay here with ye and a few others, waiting for the arrivals while Maitland heads out to gather one or two more for patrol."

Ceit glanced from one person to the next, confused. "I dinnae understand."

"I'll start," Reyna announced. "Wulf and I are going to stay back to get ourselves settled in our nice home. We are staying here on Ramsay land, but we wish to spend some time together, not in battle."

Cadyn said, "I will be doing the same with Tryana. So I will no' be going on this patrol. I may return in the future, if necessary."

Wulf added, "'Tis important to our family that we help young Perrin settle in this new world. The lad lived in the abbey for so long that becoming part of Clan Ramsay will be both confusing but exhilarating for him and for my sister and me."

Isla said, "As long as we are making promises, Grif and I are going to take a trip back to Black Isle. So we will join ye on this patrol since we are headed to Inverness, but from there we will go to spend two moons on Black Isle. I miss my sister."

Dyna said, "Ye all have good reasons, but this means that initially, we are losing Reyna, Wulf, and Cadyn. After Inverness, we will lose Isla and Grif. So we must seek out some new members to join our patrol group."

Ceit was stunned, looking from person to

person. She had to admit that she wasn't truly upset about losing Reyna and Isla since they both watched and judged her so closely, but she also didn't like the idea of losing two highly skilled archers. There would still be four of them with Ysenda and Thea, but they needed more archers. Who could possibly replace them?

Dyna then explained, "We have two new people joining us, so we will wait until they arrive. Isla and I will stay here with Ceit while we await the arrival of Wenna and Willum, daughter and son of Maggie and Will. Both are expert archers as one would expect, and Willum is also good with a sword. Ysenda and Thea, ye may choose to stay behind with us, but the others will travel with Maitland."

Maitland added, "I am going to Cameron land to approach Brin to join us. If he has any other suggestions, I will listen. If we could gain Wenna, Willum, and Brin, that would help fill in for our loss of Reyna, Wulf, Cadyn, and eventually Isla and Grif."

"So when we leave, it will be just archers?" Isla asked. "Should we no' have more swordsmen with us?"

Dyna smirked. "Well, we will have yer husband and he's a fine swordsman, but we will also have Willum. He is one verra talented man or so I'm told."

Thea smirked and said, "I havenae seen either of them in a long time. I canno' wait to meet them."

Ceit didn't know whether to be excited or upset. Was she about to be outdone, shown up, embarrassed by two more people?

But then someone else popped into her mind, and she forgot all her worries. What could be better than having the one man whom she enjoyed the most along on their patrol?

How she hoped Brin Cameron would agree to join them.

CHAPTER FIVE

BRIN SAT DOWN to break his fast, joining his father at the dais. "Da, ye are well?"

"Aye. I saw ye coming and sent the serving lass for yer porridge. She'll return shortly." His father gave him that smile that he did not trust.

"Out with it, Da. What do ye have planned for me now?" He could tell by the look on his face that he had some news for him.

"Have ye thought of anyone ye would like to court yet?"

He narrowed his gaze at his sire because he recognized that look in his sire's eyes. A bit of smugness that only he could see. His father still had a full head of hair, but strands of gray had mixed with the brown strands. His smile had become more of a crooked grin, the true sign of his attempt to connive something. "What have ye done, Da?"

The serving lass brought his porridge along with his usual honey. Neither said a word in front of the lass, but Brin's thoughts flew around in his head as he waited for her to depart. He hadn't even given it another thought until just now.

Why would his parents not let it be? He'd find his wife in his own good time.

"Go ahead. She's gone now. Tell me what ye did."

His father gave him his half-hearted shrug. "I've chosen for ye. If ye dinnae give me a name within a fortnight, I'll be announcing yer betrothal to Jocosa Gibbon. Her sire has been a loyal member of Clan Cameron for as long as I can recall. Her mother is English, but that is of no concern. She's a pretty lass."

"She is barely twenty summers!" He knew of the lass and he didn't wish to tell his sire what he'd heard about her. The lass enjoyed a quick toss in the hay of the stable with two different stable lads, or so he'd been told.

"She will give ye many bairns then. As ye know, a man can father bairns well into his sixth or seventh decade. But the mother must be young. Jocosa has strong hips. She'll give ye many fine bairns."

Brin shoveled the porridge into his mouth as quickly as he could. He didn't know what to say. He wasn't used to denying his father completely. In the past, he'd always considered Brin's thoughts on any subject. Not this one, apparently. "Does it matter to ye at all if she pleases me?" He didn't look at his father when he made that scathing comment.

"Of course, it does. In time, she will please ye; in fact, ye may learn to love each other. Many are forced to marry. My mother was forced to marry my sire and they grew to care for each other. Ye and Jocosa will do the same."

"So the Grant rule of choosing yer spouse is thrown into the wind from atop the highest mountain in the Highlands?" Brin asked, now glaring at his father. He knew what his mother would say, but he had to admit, he'd surprised him with this. He had to wonder if his mother was aware of this fated match. "Or have ye forgotten that Mama is a Grant?"

One thing he knew for certain. Brin would *not* be marrying Jocosa Gibbon.

The door to the keep opened and Maitland Menzie entered. Brin couldn't have been more grateful for the timing. "Maitland," he hollered. "Join me for some porridge."

Alaric and Tevis came in behind him, so Brin called to the serving lass to bring some bread and cheese on a platter for the group. He didn't know why they were here, but he didn't care. He had to get his father to change the subject, and Maitland's arrival couldn't have been more perfect.

His mother came down the staircase at the same time. "Maitland, I'm so pleased to see you again. We'll find ye a quick repast."

"Already taken care of, Jennie," his father said.

The group moved to a larger table where the serving lass could set down platters of food. "Maitland, what brings ye here this morn?"

"Greetings, Chief," Maitland said as he approached the table. "Pleased to see ye too, Brin. Ye are the reason we are here."

The group sat at the table, all waiting for his

mother to sit before they took their seats. "Lady Cameron, ye look lovely as usual."

Tevis said, "Greetings, Grandmama, Grandda." Son of Torcall and Riley Massie, he traveled off of Black Isle for the patrol.

Alaric Grant said, "Aunt Jennie, Uncle Aedan, we're glad to be here. There's a wee storm brewing outside. Winter is nearly upon us."

"I feel it in my bones," his mother said. "We have plenty for ye this morn, and some to take along with ye. Where are ye headed?"

"Inverness," Maitland explained. "Logan received word that King Robert wanted us to follow up on rumors of an English garrison stirring trouble in the north, so we are headed that way. Isla and Grif wish to visit her parents so they'll meet us along the way, then stay for a moon or two through winter."

"Oh, I wish they had all come along with ye," his mother said. "I so enjoy seeing all the young ones from our clans."

Maitland explained, "Dyna is staying with Ceit until she is healed, then they will meet us so we can travel together."

"Ceit?" Brin said, just a wee bit too enthusiastically if he were to guess. His concern was more than usual and his parents would not miss it, if he were to wager. "What happened with Ceit? Is she ill?" He decided he didn't care one bit if his parents noticed. He had to find out what was going on with Ceit.

His father noticed, a smug smile growing on his face. His mother contained hers, that odd look she got when she tried to hide her emotions now evident.

"We were at the Borderlands protecting a small village from an attack by English reivers. She took a blade to her thigh. She'll be fine. We brought her back to Aunt Brenna as quickly as we could."

"'Tis a good thing ye got her back to my sister's capable hands quickly to keep the fever away. Did she need stitching too?"

"She did," Maitland said. "I'm sure she will be good as new in three days. Dyna plans to join us with Thea and Ysenda too. But you know yer sister. She wouldnae allow Ceit to travel yet."

Brin asked, "No Reyna? Wulf?"

"Nay, they are staying back for the next couple of patrols along with Cadyn. They wish to be there with Perrin and help the boy get acclimated to his new home and family. 'Tis a wise plan for them, I believe."

Tevis jumped in. "And we have two new archers joining us. Wenna and Willum. Dyna is waiting for them to arrive."

"That makes up for two, but ye are losing three for now, and five once ye leave Inverness." Aedan glanced from one face to the next, all three sets of eyes now falling on Brin.

It didn't take long for both his parents to catch on, two frowns now covering their faces.

Maitland looked at him and said, "We came in the hopes that Brin could join us for this patrol. What say ye, Brin?"

Brin didn't hesitate. "I'd be glad to assist."

His mother's face fell. "Brin, are ye sure? Ye

could be stuck on Black Isle for a moon or two with winter coming. And Yule will be here before ye know it."

His father gave him that look and said, "I think Brin should stay here for the winter. With all the English garrisons around, we need to make sure the abbey is well protected."

Brin stood and said, "I'd be glad to join ye. I'll be back before ye have any trouble, Da. Besides, I can make a quick visit to see my sisters. Anything ye'd like me to take along, Mama?"

His mother bolted from her chair. "Aye, I made some clothing for the bairns. Tara's lads are still young and they go through clothing so quickly. And I have a nice gown for her daughter. Give me some time to wrap them." Tara and Shaw had lost one bairn and waited until they tried to have more, but then Tara gave birth to three in a row.

Maitland said, "There is no hurry. We'll stay a night or two if ye dinnae mind. Take yer time preparing, Brin. And we're all for the great Cameron cook's food to send us off on our journey."

His mother said, "Brin can pack some dried meat and cheese for ye all to take along."

"We'd appreciate that. Once the snow falls, pickings are slim in the forests."

Brin was pleased with the distraction. Visiting his sisters was the one reason he knew he could get his mother's support for going on patrol. He stood and said, "I'll go grab a few things for the journey."

"Take yer time," Maitland said. "Ye have a day or two."

Brin knew that, but he wished to pack before his sire forbade the trip. He strode across the great hall headed for the staircase, then took the stairs two at a time, mentally thinking of all he would need.

He wasn't in his chamber long before his sire came in, closing the door behind him. "Brin, I know what ye are doing."

"I think I'm going on patrol to protect the land of the Scots, Da. What do ye think I am doing?" He continued to toss a few things into the center of his bed while his father crossed his arms and leaned against the hearth.

"Ye are evading my dictate."

"Yer dictate?" His voice came out louder than he anticipated, but he didn't mind one bit, though he saw the shock on his sire's face.

His mother stepped inside, paling immediately. "Ye two are arguing." She held out a small container of the ointment she often used for wounds. "I brought ye yer ointment. And I have a package of clothing for the lads on Black Isle." Her face fell to the floor, the same look she always got whenever they argued, though it was rare. He respected his father's opinion on everything but who he should choose as his wife.

"Jennie, he needs to marry. I would like to forbid any travel until he's chosen a bride." Aedan crossed his arms and waited for his wife to respond.

She didn't hesitate. "Nay, Aedan. Brin is a fine

young man, and he will find the one for him in his own way." To his surprise, his mother squared her shoulders and lifted her chin when she spoke to her husband.

How grateful he was that his mother was raised to believe she had value as a woman and equal value in a marriage, an unpopular opinion by most.

"How can he when he is no' around enough to court any lass?" His sire's voice grew louder as he spoke. He took two steps toward his mother, but Brin could stand no more.

"Da, I dinnae wish for the two of ye to argue over me. I am going on this venture because I was asked to do my duty as a Scot. 'Tis right for me to go. I promise when I return from patrol, I will consider yer request and search for my betrothed on my own. And my wife will no' be Jocosa Gibbon."

His mother scowled. "Jocosa? Why would yer wife be Jocosa? Jocosa Gibbon?" She glanced from her husband back to him.

"I'm going to the stable to ready my mount. I'll chat with Maitland on our path to Inverness, make sure he has chosen the best path." He leaned over and kissed his mother's cheek. "My thanks for the ointment."

He headed out of the chamber, down the passageway. By the time he reached the staircase, he heard his mother ask, "Jocosa Gibbon? What does he speak of, Aedan? Know ye what is going on in his mind? I surely would no' choose Jocosa for him."

If he were there, he was quite sure he would see his father's eyes roll. But he heard his response loud and clear.

"Jennie, I was just trying to scare the lad. He needs to find a lass, and running around the Highlands is no' the right way to go about finding a wife."

"Mayhap 'tis Brin's way to find a wife. Leave him be. Please."

Brin smiled. He had an inkling his sire had been bluffing.

His mother was usually the wiser of the two. Was she right about this journey? Would this be Brin's way to find his wife?

A pair of green eyes and soft pink lips popped up in his head.

This could be a wonderful patrol if Ceit joined them.

CHAPTER SIX

CEIT WANDERED OUT toward the archery field. She was nearly there when her grandfather suddenly appeared next to her.

"How do ye fare, Ceit? Are ye ready for more battles yet?" The sun was out that day, showing how much white her grandfather had threaded throughout his dark blond hair.

She peered at the man she admired so, his green eyes that were all-knowing and all-seeing, the wind-tossed, wavy long hairs that showed shades of white, blond, and gray, all mixed together. The crooked grin that she adored. "Much better, Grandda. I hope we leave on the morrow."

In fact, the only thing that had dulled over the years was a wee bit of his hearing, though he vehemently denied it.

His gaze narrowed. "Ye are anxious for this patrol. Why? Willum? I hear all the lasses are excited to meet Willum. Ye met him not so long ago. He should no' be a surprise for anyone. He's family as are all the others."

"Not quite, and ye know it, Grandda. Maggie is adopted, so anyone could marry Wenna or

Willum. New faces for those of us who have lived here forever. We like new faces."

"Hmph," he grumbled. "I dinnae see ye with Willum."

"I dinnae see me with him either, but there are other lasses on patrol." She crossed her arms and looked at the man as he studied the group they approached, all practicing their archery skills.

"Mayhap Ysenda or Thea. Hmmm."

"Grandda, may I ask ye a question?"

"Of course. If 'tis worthy of an answer, I'll give it. If no', I'll ignore ye."

"The same as always." She giggled and he winked at her.

"Who is the best archer on the patrol now that Reyna is gone?"

He whirled to face her, his gaze locked on her. "Why do ye ask?"

"Just curious."

"Granddaughter, ye answer me with shite from bulls yet ye wish me to tell ye true?"

She blushed at that. "Please, Grandda."

"Look, I know Gwynie said I made a big mistake by calling ye the best of the archers when I teased Grif. But ye were the best then. 'Tis the truth that there are quite a few of ye that are highly skilled, and whoever is best will depend on the battle. The time. The moon and its cycles. All of those things can affect an archer as ye well know. Ye are as good as or better than Reyna, Isla, Ysenda, and Thea. I will wager ye are as good as Wenna and Willum, but each battle, each battle site, each enemy is different. Ye will be the best in one battle, and Thea will be best at the next. Dinnae worry yer head about being the best. It doesnae matter. Be the best ye can be, and dinnae worry about the others."

"Dammit, Grandda. Just answer the simple question."

"I did. And dinnae curse at me, lass."

She sighed, then turned to the tiny voice behind her. "Grandpapa, will ye no' set me on yer shoulders so I can practice my archery?"

Her five-year-old sister came directly in front of her grandsire and stopped. "I need yer help, Grandpapa. Please?"

Her grandfather chuckled and bent over to lift the wee lass and toss her into the air. "How is that, my sweet one? 'Tis high enough for ye to see?"

Lainey giggled incessantly as her doting grandfather tossed her into the air four times before setting her down. "Please, Grandpapa? I can see better from yer shoulders."

"Grandda has a sore shoulder, Lainey. Leave him be. Ye can stand on that boulder over there like ye've done before." Her sister had a way of manipulating her grandfather better than anyone else, her golden hair plaited perfectly, her dimples deepened with her phony smile.

Her grandfather gave her a sheepish grin and said, "Och, 'tis much better now. Here, lassie. I'll help ye."

The man lifted the lass, stifling his groan of pain until she settled the way she liked. "Over there,

Grandpapa. Over there with Wenna! I wish to shoot next to my new friend."

Ceit shook her head, watching her grandfather do whatever her sister asked without any argument. She was the bairn of the family at present, so she wasn't surprised. Though Lainey had held the prized spot for a while since neither her mother nor Merewen had plans for any new bairns. Molly and Maggie were also done having bairns, so the only one who could have another was probably Brigid.

"Logan, ye have a bad shoulder," her grandmother shouted at him. "Put the lass down." Her dear grandmother was almost always at the archery field, even though her vision had deteriorated over the years.

"She's fine, Gwynie."

"Ye spoil Lainey too much."

"Nay more than any other," he bellowed at his wife.

Ceit nearly said, "I would disagree, Grandda. But Lainey is having the time of her life."

She decided to keep her mouth closed, instead going over the words her grandfather had told her. Did it depend on the battle? The weather? The site?

She didn't doubt that it mattered if a lass was in the middle of her bleeding time. That often made her feel weak, though it never seemed to bother Ysenda. Some it did, others it didn't.

Her grandmother sidled over next to her. "Are ye ready to go on patrol or do ye wish to sit this one out?"

"Nay, I must go, Grandmama. Dyna and Maitland are losing five already. I'll be fine."

Her grandmother crossed her arms and looked across the field. "Ye know I can barely see that small target from here. It's disappeared. Can ye still see it?"

Ceit stared at the targets at the far end of the field. "I can see them all from here."

"As good as ye used to?"

She took five steps forward. "Aye. I can see them just fine." She didn't look into her grandmother's eyes when she told that wee lie.

Her grandmother turned to look at her, brushing stray hairs from her plait. "I dinnae believe ye, but I'm sure yer sight is no' as bad as mine is, so ye'll be fine. Mine left me gradually too. I hardly noticed it at first, but each year, it grew a wee bit worse. Ye can do other things besides be a skilled archer, but I think ye know that."

"For instance?"

"Ye can teach archery. Or ye could teach young ones to read, a most important skill. Ye could become a healer like yer Aunt Brenna. Ye could marry and have bairns of yer own, spend yer time raising them and teaching them archery. I'll no' be able to teach the Ramsay lasses forever. Someone must take my place."

"Mayhap later."

"Ceit, have ye yer eye on anyone?"

"Nay. I doubt I'll ever marry."

Her grandmother looked shocked. "Why would ye say that? I thought myself much like ye, but even I found that ornery man over there."

"Ye mean the one ye adore? Because," she said, deciding it was time to explain her feelings to someone. "There is no one here on Ramsay land for me, and I'll never leave Clan Ramsay. So my future is already set. I'm bound to this land."

"Truly? No Ramsay guard has caught yer eye? Well then, marry a Grant. There are plenty of them, and ye are no' true blood with most of them. Or what about Lewis from Clan Matheson? Why not live with Aunt Brigid on Black Isle?"

"Nay. I'd never go that far away."

The woman broke into a hearty laugh. "Ye just wait, lass. Ye havenae met the right one yet, have ye? When ye do, ye'll know it."

She scowled. "I dinnae think so, Grandmama. I wish to never marry."

"Ye'll see."

Confused, she wasn't going to let her grandmother go without an explanation. "I dinnae understand what ye mean. How will I know it?"

"When ye know ye'd follow him to England and back, then ye'll know he's the one for ye. Ye'll fall madly in love with him then."

She didn't say the words in her mind, just nodded.

She was never falling in love with any man, and if she did, she'd never marry him. That would mean she'd have to leave Ramsay land and she couldn't do that. This was the only place where women were truly valued as archers, where being born a lass did not mean you'd be stuck delivering bairns and sewing tapestries for the rest of your days.

She wished to go on patrol, see the world, participate in battle, do something worth remembering. Her main desire was to earn the same reputation her dear grandmother had, and the only way to do that was to get her guidance along the way. If she left Ramsay land, she'd be giving up on her dreams.

Never. She was never leaving Clan Ramsay.

CHAPTER SEVEN

BRIN COULDN'T HAVE been happier taking his leave from Cameron Castle. The group rode together past the abbey, checking in briefly and saying goodbye to his uncle Ruari. He was hoping to find some excitement on patrol. "Think ye we will have a skirmish or two, Maitland?"

"I'm sure we will."

Alaric said, "We've had more than I thought we would. That last one was the one that upset me the most. Those poor lasses."

Brin looked from Alaric to Maitland. "The one Ceit was injured in?"

"Aye," Maitland explained. "English bastards were abusing three young lassies in front of their families. I dinnae like it." Maitland's voice turned deeper than usual.

Tevis said, "We all knew ye could no' let the bastards go. Mighty bold of them to do. I wish I knew how they caught the Scots off-guard the way they did. They were no' that skilled."

"One of them told me they'd just lost a bairn to the fever. Said they were no' paying attention.

Ye canno' let yer guard down ever. They learned from it," Maitland added. "I hope we dinnae find any more situations like that. They were just reivers, I believe."

Brin said, "And now we go after a group of English marauders? Not a cavalry?"

"Not a cavalry," Maitland stated. "Every few years this happens. The English come after the Scots and all our beautiful castles. Ye are lucky ye have no' had many of the reivers here, Brin."

"None that I recall. Not in the last two score years or more."

"Yer sire has done a great job protecting yer land, Brin. Has he had many battles around here? Any at your neighboring clans?" Maitland asked.

"None that I know of. 'Tis no' hard defending our land. There have rarely been many threats that I'm aware of." He shrugged his shoulders. Thinking of taking over his rightful job as heir to the chieftain had never bothered him. To him it would be a simple job. No one ever dared to challenge the Camerons or the abbey. In fact, it was partly the reason he liked to leave on patrol. Gives him some excitement in his life.

"I wouldn't relax too much, Brin. Lochluin Abbey has a reputation of holding many treasures. They've been attacked multiple times over the years. Look at the time just before yer parents married. I heard it was a terrible attack."

"Aye, I've heard of that one, but no' many serious ones since then. Tell me more about where we are headed on this patrol." He didn't wish to hear about how hard it was to defend

Cameron Castle. He'd lived there for years and knew better than anyone. The truth was it wasn't difficult at all.

He wanted a challenge.

"Word is that there is a group of rogue English reivers going through the Highlands. Last word was they were headed toward Inverness."

"Where is Dyna and her group?"

"We will meet them near one of the favored Grant caves. A good place to spend the night before heading into the wild lands near Inverness. If we dinnae catch them, we will move on to Black Isle to see what they've learned."

They'd been traveling for most of the day and seen little of interest. The path had been clear and they hadn't seen any evidence of a larger group traveling.

"Will we make it to the Grant cave this eve?"

"Aye, we should. Just before dusk. Ye are looking for someone?" Maitland asked, peering at him with an odd expression. "Hoping to see someone?"

He thought for a moment but then dodged the question. "Aye, my sisters on Black Isle. I've not seen them in a while."

Maitland barked out a chortle. "Ye know who I'm thinking on. I saw ye with her before."

He stared at Maitland, unable to believe anyone had figured out who he was interested in.

"Ye and Ceit? Do ye think no one noticed?" Maitland barked a laugh. "I noticed. And I'm sure others did too."

"I like Ceit, but no more than that."

"Sure, Brin." Maitland turned toward Brin, his long dark hair swinging in the wind, a subtle grin on his face.

He knew what that meant, but he ignored Maitland. Unfortunately, Maitland wasn't ready to drop the subject as he'd hoped.

"Yer sire wishes to see ye married and ye know it. Think ye he will no' betroth ye to someone?" He glanced over at Brin, arching a brow. "Ye are asking for trouble if ye keep ignoring it. Chieftains have this common desire to see their sons marry so they can have grandsons. A chieftain will not sleep well if they dinnae have someone to take care of their land. He'll find ye someone."

"Nay, he is bluffing." He believed his father would never do such a thing. At least, he always believed it before this last time. His sire was getting more insistent about it.

"Ye are the only male heir to the Cameron chieftainship. And even if ye wished to have one of yer sisters take it over, neither one lives on Cameron land. 'Tis all on yer shoulders, Brin, and dinnae try to dodge it. Take yer rightful place as chieftain and find a lass to love and marry. Ye have a duty to yer clan even if ye wish to ignore it."

"I'll probably find one to marry, just to make my parents happy. Make them leave me be."

"Ye've had plenty of time to find one to love. Ye'll be much happier in a marriage if ye love her too."

"That will never happen. I tried loving once and she rejected me. So I may marry for my parents, but I'll never allow myself to fall in love."

Maitland cast him a sideways glance, then shook his head as if to disagree with him totally. But Brin knew Maitland's background, and he was doing the same as Brin.

Maitland said, "Ye were too young. Ye were in lust, not love. Find the right one. Ye'll no' regret it. Mayhap 'tis Ceit MacAdam."

"Menzie, ye are avoiding marriage as much as I am. Ye fell in love once and lost as I did. So how can ye judge me? I dinnae wish to be hurt like that again." His voice reached a tone that let Maitland know that this was now a serious conversation.

"Ye make a fair point that I canno' argue. If ye wish to hear the truth, I hate myself sometimes for no' seeking out another partner, but it feels wrong. I was married, ye were no'. I do think it makes a difference. I feel as if falling in love with another will be betraying my wife. I canno' shake that feeling. I canno' argue with ye, so I'll ask ye to please reconsider."

Brin nodded, not wishing to continue the conversation where they were. It was a conversation for another time. "I'll consider yer words."

"All I ask is that ye be open to loving another lass."

"And I'd ask the same of ye, Maitland. Ye've lived with yer pain for long enough. 'Tis time to consider some happiness in yer life."

They rode on a bit without any conversation, Brin heavy in his thoughts about his life and all he'd wished it to be. But it had not turned out that way.

"Slow, Alaric," Maitland instructed to the man in front of him. "The cave is up ahead to the left. We must check to see if Dyna is there."

"I'll go. I know it best," Alaric replied, sending his horse on ahead of the others before taking a turn off the main path.

He wasn't gone long before he returned, waving his hand at the group. "They're here. Just sitting down to roast a pheasant they caught."

Brin smiled, pleased at the thought of meat for this meal. He tired of dried meat when traveling and the aroma of the roasted pheasant carried to them as they headed down the side path.

They approached the group and Brin dismounted, glancing across the group and sorting out the two he didn't know. Once they joined the group, Maitland made introductions to Wenna and Willum to their group. Then he added, "I'm guessing Willum caught the pheasant."

"Nay, Willum caught two rabbits, but it was Ceit who nailed the pheasant," Dyna declared. "And we are all grateful."

Wenna added, "And I found the pear tree with several still firm at the top." She pointed to a small sack full of apples and pears.

"I'll take a pear, if ye dinnae mind. 'Tis my favorite autumn fruit," Brin said, catching Ceit's eye. He noticed she was also enjoying the same juicy fruit. Tempted as he was to watch her sweet lips, he turned away before he could embarrass himself.

They joined the group gathered around the small fire, chatting about the weather, the trip, and the ones they were losing. Wenna was a beauty with her dark hair plaited in an unusual way, but she looked young compared to the others along with them. Willum was the tallest in the group, his dark hair and broad shoulders making him the image of his sire.

After they finished eating and the group broke apart, he moved over to Ceit to check on her injury. "Greetings to ye, Ceit. I heard ye took a sword to yer leg. How is it healing?"

She glanced down at the soft leggings she wore, only one small spot of blood seeped through the soft fabric. "'Tis nearly healed. Grandmama gave me her best leggings because of my injury. I love the color, a red nearly dark enough to hide the blood, though I've not leaked much. 'Tis much better, but the stitches pull occasionally. I'm to have Jennet remove them when we arrive on Black Isle."

"I'm shocked that you caught the blade. Tell me about the battle." Her golden hair was plaited and it went nearly to her waist. Many admired her for that alone, but what attracted Brin was the green and gold in her eyes. If he looked close enough, the gold flecks danced as if sparks from a fire in the middle of a lush summer forest. Her high cheekbones and the pinkest lips he'd ever seen called to him like a siren. But she lost that glow as soon as he mentioned the battle. He was definitely interested in hearing it from her point of view. How difficult did she find it to kill a man? Was it different for lasses?

"Not much to tell, Brin." She shrugged. "A group of bullies decided to burn down a small village of Scots just over the border. We didnae agree with them. There were women and bairns and in the center were three bastards groping young lasses. Other men carrying torches approached the group of huts. We had to stop them. I didnae wish to take any chances so when the opportunity arose, I rushed around the English with the hope of freeing the bindings on the Scots. Paid the price with a sword from the last standing reiver. But we won in the end."

"Had to hurt, lass," he said in such a low voice. He wished she would lean her head on his shoulder and allow him to comfort her, take in her sweet scent. She had the oddest way of smelling like pine and mint together. "How could ye bear it?"

"It did hurt, though it took a few moments to settle on me. The chaos was more than I was used to. I didnae handle it well." She dropped her gaze but he noticed the others were watching the two of them, so he changed the topic.

"How is yer brother doing with his new wife? And yer wee sister? What is her name?"

"Ye mean Lainey?" Ceit laughed. "She is fine. She chases after Grandpapa to get him to bend to her will."

"Logan? I dinnae see that happening often." Logan was a strong-minded warrior. Even though he was in his older years, his mind was quick as anyone's.

"Lainey has him wrapped around her wee finger and her toes. Whatever she asks for, she gets. He puts her on his shoulders then he complains about shoulder pain for the entire day and night. Anything for wee Lainey."

"Are ye a wee bit jealous of the attention she gets?" He couldn't stop the smile from crossing his face though he hoped she wouldn't take offense by it. The image of the old warrior doing whatever a wee lass wanted was appealing.

"Nay. I feel bad for her sometimes. She is the only one left of that age. We all grew up together. Cadyn, me, Ysenda, Errol, Padean, Drystan, Thea. She is the wee babe of the family for now."

Brin had the odd urge to push her to find out more about where she was at in her life's journey. Whether it was the green of her eyes or the softness of her skin that caused it, he wasn't sure. But he shared his thoughts in a subtle way, or so he thought.

"Then why do ye no' marry and leave Ramsay land? Sounds as though ye would be much happier." He hadn't expected that he would be holding his breath for her answer.

Would Ceit consider marrying him and moving to Clan Cameron?

CHAPTER EIGHT

CEIT STOPPED SHORT, frowned, then looked up at him. "I'll never marry. I've vowed no' to."

She could see how her answer surprised Brin. "Truly? Why no'? Is that no' every lasses dream?"

Being a wee bit stubborn as her grandsire often told her, she crossed her arms and replied, "I dinnae know. Is that no' every lad's dream?" She couldn't stop her lower lip from pushing out, showing that pout that her mother often called her on with a sharp bark of her name. But since her mother was not here, she could pout all she wished. And she hadn't liked the idea that Brin had suggested that lasses were simpleminded enough to only consider marriage as their ultimate goal in life.

By the expression on his face, she guessed Brin decided to leave that subject alone, instead appealing to the connection they had. "Would ye like to stroll a bit to see if yer leg is healing?"

"Aye," she replied rather quickly, pushing herself to a standing position before he could reach to assist her. "I can do it myself."

He grinned.

Dyna approached them from the forest. "Never try to help Ceit, Brin. Keep yer distance. Take her for a walk though. 'Tis good to keep moving her wound."

Brin nodded, saying nothing about Ceit's stubbornness though he was probably thinking on it. Her sire always called her stubborn, and often added "too stubborn for a lass." But she did not change her thinking because of something her father said. She couldn't change who she was.

Once they were alone, he asked her a question that took her by surprise. "Truly, ye dinnae wish to marry?"

She shrugged, wondering why he would pose such an odd question, but then said, "I doubt I ever will. But ye wish to?"

"Nay, I dinnae wish to but I'll be forced to marry eventually since I'm heir to the chieftainship. Da has already warned me that if I dinnae find someone soon then he'll choose for me." She noticed how he tensed on the subject. This was definitely a sore spot for Brin, but he was quite a bit older than she was. He was heir to the chieftain so it didn't surprise her any. He'd waited a long time to marry. She couldn't help but wonder about it, but after his reaction, she would not ask his reasons.

"And ye havenae found someone yet, I'm assuming."

"I did." He paused, apparently considering his words before he continued. She was surprised that he put that much thought into his words.

"I fell in love once, but she chose another. So

I'm no longer interested. I'll probably never fall for another lass, but I'll marry someday." That was much more than she expected him to admit. He'd been rejected and it still hurt, something she'd never experienced.

No one had considered her as a suitable partner. She had to laugh at the irony of their opposing positions. "'Tis the opposite of me. I'll probably fall in love but I'll never marry."

"But why?" He tipped his head, his strong jawline highlighted by the fire. His beard had come in a wee bit and she found it quite attractive. His coloring was quite dark like the Grants.

She shrugged her shoulder. It was hard to explain her position. "Ye see, Clan Ramsay is the primary clan known for archery, and the only clan willing to train their women as much as their men. The only clan willing to allow their women to fight alongside the men. I'll be an archer my entire life. Why would I ever move to another clan? I'd never be allowed to do what I love."

"Ye truly love battle?"

He had to know that Clan Ramsay was known for its female warriors, more specifically its female archers. "Aye, I love going to battle. I love being an archer, taking part in competitions too." In any other clan, she'd be busy weaving tapestries and having bairns. Neither one sounded appealing to her. "And reading. Besides the clans with Grant women, no one else believes in teaching the average woman how to read. How daft is that belief?"

"I canno' argue with ye there. My mother made

sure I could read at a young age, but Tara taught me. Tara and Riley taught many in the clan. And my sire goes to the abbey every once in a while to see about having books delivered. He loves to read too."

"There ye have it. I dinnae wish to marry into a clan that does not value their women or allow them to read."

"What about a guard in yer clan? Is there no' someone closer ye would consider marrying?"

"Nay, I've already considered them all and none suit me." She wished to change the subject, anything but talk about her interest in men. "Are ye headed to Black Isle to see yer sisters? Helping us along the way for a short time only?"

"Nay, my sisters have busy lives. They dinnae need me around. They are content with their families, taking care of their bairns. Tara is still a healer and loves it. She claims all of the clans on Black Isle now come to Clan Matheson when they need a healer."

"Truly?"

"Aye, she learned from my mother. Aunt Brigid and Aunt Jennet learned from Aunt Brenna. Those three could talk about healing for hours, though Brigid prefers to deliver bairns."

"Then who will be the next healer for yer clan? I know Aunt Brenna wished for Jennet to stay on at Clan Ramsay for that reason. Though she says little, I dinnae think she was so happy when Jennet fell in love and married on Black Isle."

"No one has taken on the art of healing yet. My mother hasnae trained anyone else. My mother will live for many more years, but after that, who knows what will happen? I hope when I'm chieftain, I can convince someone to join the clan. Or convince Tara to return."

"Mayhap Tara will return someday."

"Ye see of what I speak. They are all Ramsays and Camerons and they fell in love with someone on Black Isle. Tara asks for books because she still loves to read. I hear Riley spends most of her time teaching the wee ones. Others will discover the value in reading."

"True, but mostly for the lads. Will they feel the same about lasses?"

"I surely hope so. 'Twould be ignorant no' to teach both." They'd strolled quite a distance away, and he stopped and turned to face her, something that caught her by surprise.

"Would ye consider kissing one who ye will never marry?" His gaze locked on hers and she was mesmerized, his white teeth bright even in the beginning of dusk.

Ceit gave him a puzzled look, but then he leaned closer and whispered, "I meant me, since I'll never fall in love and ye will never marry. Doesnae mean we canno' play a wee bit, does it no'? Or are ye no' interested?"

She'd kissed a few before, but she hadn't found all that slobbering a bit appealing. But Brin was different, and it couldn't hurt to do some exploring while she was away from home, away from prying eyes and tattling tongues. Nodding her agreement, his lips descended on hers and after a moment she found she had a new interest in her life.

Brin Cameron.

His lips were warm and soft at first, but that changed as soon as she pressed her body against his, melting her curves against the hard planes of his well-toned physique. She wasn't quite steady enough on her feet to risk a fall from her wound, so she let him support her.

And how well he did.

His mouth angled over hers, teasing her lips until she parted for him with a sigh, giving him entrance to a place no one else had been. She'd never wanted anyone else this close. His tongue reached out to hers and she nearly started, so surprised by this act.

But what surprised her even more was that she liked it. Kissing Brin was different, exciting. Being in his arms sent odd desires through her, the kind she'd only heard others speak of, not anything she'd ever experienced before. She mimicked his actions, teasing him with her tongue until he groaned, clutching her close to his body so she could feel every part of his hardness, his strength, his size overpowering her senses. But an odd part of their encounter gave her a power she didn't know she had.

The power to entice a man just by the taste of her lips.

Brin tasted of pear and pheasant, a combination she found appealing even though she'd just eaten the same. The taste of the man was so appealing that odd flutters found their way through her insides—to her belly, her chest, even odd sensations in her female parts. What exactly was this all about?

Was this that strange thing her mother had often taunted her about? That women had the power over men, they just rarely knew how to use it. Her mother liked to suggest that it was this power that made her father jump over the cliff for her.

But then the worst happened. In tugging her closer, Brin pressed against her wound and she involuntarily jolted, a piercing pain shooting through her.

He knew it too.

"Och, yer wound. I'm so sorry." He set her back carefully.

Struggling to stay upright, she gritted her teeth as the pain abated. But her balance was due more to her reaction to him and not at all due to her wound.

She'd never tell him how she felt at that very moment. Enchanted. Intrigued. Definitely wanting more of this newfound emotion that she struggled to identify, but she doubted it would ever happen with anyone else. This would happen only with Brin. She didn't understand why, but she was certain of it, and under no circumstance would she tell him that truth.

Maitland interrupted them, calling to them as he approached. "'Tis nearly dark so we're settling down. I wish to rise early and get on our way. I hope to be close to Inverness by the next nightfall.

I feel winter in the air, and I am no' the only one. We canno' afford to slow our journey."

Brin nodded to him, not saying a word, instead placing his hand at the small of Ceit's back, something she liked.

Maitland stopped, studied the two of them, then turned around and led the way back so they could not see his face when he uttered his next statement over his shoulder.

"Ye two might wish to take yer time returning. Ye both look thoroughly kissed and ye canno' hide it."

Ceit was pleased he couldn't see her blush.

Brin said something completely different as the wind picked up. "Forget about us, Menzie. There is definitely a storm on the horizon. The only question is how long before it drops on us."

"'Tis too early for snow," Maitland said.

"In the Highlands, 'tis never too early for snow."

Ceit didn't like the sound of that at all. She had the oddest feeling of impending doom.

But she'd not say a word because she was starting to enjoy this patrol better than any other, just because of Brin Cameron.

The doom disappeared.

CHAPTER NINE

B RIN HATED THE fact that he'd been right.
It was never too early for snow, and the light
flakes that appeared in the crisp air above them
took nearly all of them by surprise. All but Brin,
Dyna, and Alaric.

Dyna said, "These types of storms seem to
come out of nowhere and drop heavy snow
quickly. Because 'tis no' truly cold yet, it drops
heavy snow, the kind that sticks to the ground
and causes avalanches when in a ravine. We need
to get through that ravine ahead quickly. Once
we've made it past there, we can make it to Black
Isle quick enough, weather the storm out there."

"Good idea," Maitland said. "I prefer to be near
a hearth with a warm bowl of pottage during a
snowstorm."

The snow started light but came in heavier
than Brin expected. Before long, he was moving
closer to his group just to chat. "We'll need to
hurry or we'll never get past the ravine. It's not
just about an impending avalanche. The ground
is covered with snow already and ye know what
that means."

Dyna said, "I canno' believe the ground isnae warmer. It should have melted the snow. It shouldn't stick for another hour."

"I agree, but that's not what the ground is saying. It's turned slick already so that means horses have trouble staying on the path," Brin said.

Alaric said, "'Tis just ahead. A wee bit off the main path but easy to find. If we canno' make it across the ravine, we have the cave. 'Tis nearly upon us."

"Ye dinnae wish to stop at the cave?" Grif asked. He knew the area better than anyone since he was from Black Isle. "Mayhap we should wait out the storm."

"And then we risk freezing to death," Alaric said. "'Tis my experience that men hold up in the cold better than women. We have several along with us, and I hate to think of them in the cave in the middle of a storm. Ye know as well as I do that if they are thin they have trouble holding their heat."

"Be careful what ye say about the female constitution. Many are as tough as any of us," Grif said.

Dyna added, "He's right, Grif. I know ye stand up for yer wife, but when it comes to holding up in cold temperatures, men are like warm hearths compared to women. 'Tis the way we are made."

Alaric nodded. "I think we push through."

"The ravine is close enough to try. I'm hoping half the group can get through. That way, they can return to help clear it when the storm ends. If we dinnae all make it through the ravine, some of us may have to shelter there until the storm finishes and we can pass again, but I'm hoping we can all get through first." Dyna turned. "'Twill be much better if we can make it to Matheson land by traveling the coastline. The snow is light around the water."

Brin said, "Let Grif lead. He knows the route and the dangers. I'll take the rear." He moved his horse back once the group arranged themselves in single file to attempt the pass.

The group was large in number since they traveled with Isla and Grif still—twelve total. Brin was behind Ceit at the rear of the group as they approached the ravine. A whorl of snow came out of the sky, the wind blurring their view while they arranged themselves as they approached the ravine.

Dyna yelled back, "I thought it was just ahead but we are a bit south of it. We must keep moving quickly or we may not get through."

Brin agreed with her announcement simply because he didn't wish to be in the cave for a two-day snowstorm either. Ceit glanced back at him warily and he waved at her. "Keep moving. We have to get through that ravine or we'll be spending a few nights in a cave."

She yelled back, "I've only heard nightmares about being caught in a cave during a snowstorm. Aunt Maddie nearly died in one so they say."

"Good reason to keep moving."

Brin dropped his face down as the wind whipped through again, heavy snow now filling the air with mesmerizing swirls. The wind dropped the temperature so much that it took his breath away. "Ceit, use yer scarf."

The lasses all wore scarves once the leaves turned, but he had none, instead depending on the ability to wrap his plaid over his head if necessary. Grateful he'd thought to wear his wool mantle instead of his heavy plaid, the extra fabric at his neck was already drenched. He hunched his shoulders into the wool, praying the storm was short-lived as they often were, especially this early in the season.

Ceit slowed her horse as they approached the ravine, stopping short of the end. "Mayhap we should wait in the cave for a bit."

The other horses had already moved quite a ways across the ravine. "Go, Ceit. Ye are losing the trail. 'Tis difficult to see in this snow. The tracks will be blown away in minutes."

She plowed ahead, dipping her head low, and he brought his horse as close to hers as he dared. The snow didn't let up at all, instead the wind letting out an eerie howl through the trees that he didn't like. He prayed they would make it through.

But it wasn't meant to be.

The oddest rumbling started, and he looked up, expecting the noise to be from snow thunder, something he'd heard only on a couple of occasions, a sound he dreaded. But this was worse.

He only had a few seconds to bellow. "Ceit!" He lurched forward, grabbing onto the reins of her horse to tug them backwards, her horse stumbling but her deft skills calming the beast as it righted itself, backing up enough to miss the giant avalanche in front of them, the two of them barely out of the way.

The horse became skittish so he hopped off his horse and grabbed Ceit, tossing her onto his own. "Go! Take it back to the cave. We can still get there."

He calmed her horse enough to lead it back to the cave they'd passed, grateful that the horse had trusted him enough to follow him away from the rumbling mountain of snow, burying everything in its path with its ice-cold tendrils of heavy-laden precipitation.

Following Ceit, he was surprised to hear a bird call he recognized once the avalanche slowed. Clan Grant, Ramsay, Cameron, Menzie all used the same pattern. One to let others know you needed help, another to say you were hale.

He answered saying they were hale.

A voice bellowed deep, one he recognized as Maitland's. "Stay in the cave. We canno' get through."

Brin gave his call saying he agreed, and they were both hale. Praying the other group was safe and well past the trouble, he hoped they could make it to the water's edge soon, giving them safe travel to the Black Isle.

Once they found the cave, Brin managed to get both horses inside. It was tall enough for the beasts, though they had to duck a wee bit to get inside, but the two animals in the cave opening would help to block the snow from flying inside, making it a safer haven for all of them. The storm was no place for even a horse.

He settled the animals with some oats to make sure they wouldn't bolt, then moved to the back of the cave, grateful to see some dry wood at the back, something everyone in their clans did to guarantee there would be wood the next time someone was forced to stay inside.

"Ceit, are ye hurt at all?" he asked, piling the wood before he started the fire.

"Nay," she said, tugging her scarf off and shaking all the snow from her head. "Ye are hale?"

"I'm fine."

"Ye heard from Maitland?" She was fully aware of their bird-calling system. Logan made sure all lads and lasses were trained to communicate in the wild. Male voices usually carried better, but sometimes it was the high pitch of a lass's voice that carried best.

"Aye, said they are hale and moving forward. Said the ravine was impassible, advised us to wait the storm out in the cave. They'll be back for us. That much we know."

Ceit found a stone to hang her wet scarf on, then moved over to the horse to remove her saddle bag. "I need something dry, my leggings are drenched."

"I need a change too. I'll get the fire going and we can hang our wet things nearby to dry them. We dinnae have much wood, so we must use it well."

"Aye, turn yer head while I change, please."

He did as she asked. Normally, he would have loved to sneak a peek of her fine arse, but he was too worried to think on that. This was not a good situation. He knew there was little dry wood, and they could freeze easily.

He recalled the story about Aunt Maddie nearly freezing to death if not for divine intervention, something some didn't believe, but he did. The story was beautiful to him. Alex had been led to her cave by their grandchildren.

Their yet to be born grandchildren had interfered, locating Alex in the snow and leading him straight to Maddie. He'd had to breathe life into her, following the instructions of Dyna.

But that had been *before* Dyna was born. Maddie had been caught in a storm on the way to visit Brenna, and she was carrying Dyna's sire, Connor. Dyna had no memory of it, but it was truly a favorite of hers to retell. She loved the idea that she came to her grandparents' rescue just so her father could be born.

He shivered, saying a quick prayer that the same would not happen to him and Ceit. It was early winter and the ground was surely warm enough to melt the snow quickly. One day at most and they could take their leave.

He had to consider the fact that if the ravine were still blocked, they would have to return to Grant or Cameron land. Either one sounded wonderful at the moment.

Would they survive? It was on his shoulders.

CHAPTER TEN

CEIT CHANGED AS quickly as she could, the shivering inside of her rattling her more than she liked. What the hell were they to do? Once she finished, she wrapped a plaid around her then donned her mantle again, her fingers so cold it frightened her.

She'd been in these temperatures multiple times, but she had never had to camp overnight in such conditions. She watched as Brin struggled with the fire, his hands also shaking, and was relieved when he finally managed to spark a flame. After checking both horses and taking a quick peek outside to see nothing had changed, she moved near the fire at the back of the cave, warming her hands before shoving them inside her mantle for protection.

"Is that all the wood ye found?" Her gaze searched the area, fear overtaking her belly.

He pointed to the few small pieces he'd set aside. "Our last resort when this is done."

"Will it last long enough?" She didn't finish her sentence because her mind didn't wish to complete it.

"Aye. I dinnae think this snow will last long. We could be moving before dark."

"But 'twill be dark within the hour. We'll never move in the middle of the night."

Brin let out a loud sigh as he stared out the mouth of the cave. "It has to stop snowing first. Then it has to melt enough to drop the rest of the snow down the ravine in order for our path to be cleared. We'll need a nice sunny morn on the morrow."

"But the sun rarely hits the ravine. Who knows how long it will be. We could go back."

Brin rubbed his chin absentmindedly. "I've thought of that, but I think our best plan is to stay here until the snow lets up. Ye know how easy it is to get lost in that whirling snow. We would not be safe until the snow slows, especially in the dark of night. And I canno' believe it will last long given the timing of the season. 'Tis too early for a major snowstorm. This will pass quickly and we can move on. Once we get on the other side of the ravine, the coastline is no' far. There'll be no snow and plenty of dry wood once we make it to the edge of the river. Beauly Firth is less than two hours from the ravine. Once we are there, the rest of the trip is easy traveling. Ye know that Black Isle rarely has deep snow. 'Tis the same for the area near the firth."

"I suppose ye are correct." She had an aching feeling being apart from the rest of the group. But if she were to be stuck with anyone, she'd prefer it to be Brin.

He took his saddle bag and carried it over to

a rock. "Come sit with me and we'll have some dried meat. We need to keep our strength."

"I have some apples," she said, taking two out of her bag and offering one to Brin.

They sat close together on the rock, closer than what would be considered appropriate, but she could actually feel his heat. She'd often heard that men gave off so much heat that women snuggled against their husbands in bed. Would Brin allow her to cuddle against him this night?

He used his dagger to cut the apple, chewing slowly as if to savor it. She had to ask the obvious question. "What if we dinnae make it out?"

Brin jerked his head to face her. "Ye canno' think that way. We will make it out."

"And if we freeze like Aunt Maddie nearly did?" Everyone knew the story of her near death experience.

"Aunt Maddie was alone. 'Tis the difference. We have each other. I'll keep ye warm, ye have my word of honor."

She didn't comment, instead chewing on a piece of dried meat. "Just to make conversation, suppose we dinnae make it out. Have ye any regrets?"

"Regrets?" he asked with a surprised look on his face. "Truly? What kind of regrets do ye mean?"

"The kind that ye regret not doing something before ye die. Something ye wish ye would have done." She had her own couple of things but wasn't sure if she trusted him enough to share her inner thoughts.

"I suppose."

"I do too."

They ate in silence, but then Brin said, "I'll share one if ye share." He arched a brow at her awaiting her answer.

She stared at him, locking her gaze with his. Could she trust him with her innermost thoughts? Or would he tell all once they left? It was time to be thoughtful about what she shared of herself. "Agreed. Ye first." She grinned, glad to see her comment made him smile. Brin was a handsome man, one of the few men who set her heart afluttering just from a glance. His hair was of the darkest wood in the forest, the kind that was nearly black. His eyes were a deep blue like a midnight sky with speckles of the green of the moss here and there. Only in the flames could she see that color. He had a strong jawline and the whitest teeth ever. His smile was the kind every lass fell in love with, or so she'd heard when she'd been on Cameron land.

"All right. I regret I never married. My parents pushed me, but I never found the right lass. They were no' happy that I havenae given them a grandbairn or two yet."

"Or ten? Yer mother would like five or six at the verra least."

He glanced up at her with a shocked expression. "Aye, ye know her well." Brin reached for her hand and cocooned it inside his own, warming her in more ways than she could explain to anyone.

"Why have ye no' found anyone? Have ye

looked or just no' been interested in marriage?"
She was curious. Brin was quite a bit older than
she was so it should have occurred to him more
than once. "How many winters are ye? Ye were
born in the winter?"

"One and forty. Quite a bit older than ye, lass.
Probably twice."

"Aye, I'm two and twenty." His blue eyes
entranced her up this close. She could see every
green fleck inside.

"Och, I feel ancient now." He chuckled, a
sound that rumbled from deep within.

Why had she never noticed a man's laugh
before? Brin's appealed to her but she didn't
know why. Being this close to him brought many
new thoughts to her mind, ones she'd never had
before, but the one that was foremost would
probably haunt her. Was he attracted to her as
much as she was attracted to him?

"But ye dinnae act old at all." And he surely did
no' look it. Men had a way of hiding their years.
And he kept fit, his broad shoulders overpowering
his narrow waist.

"Many thanks to ye."

"So why have ye no' found anyone? Are ye so
fussy?"

"Nay," he barked too quickly. "I did find
someone but she refused me."

"Truly? Ye said you had been refused but
I canno' believe it." She wished to know who
this woman was and how long ago it happened
and why she would turn such a handsome man
away…she wanted to know everything.

"Believe it. Enough about me. Yer turn for confession. What do ye regret?"

Ceit chewed on her lower lip. How much should she admit? She had two different regrets, but she didn't know if she could admit one.

"Never mind. I'll guess. Ye wished to be the best archer in Clan Ramsay."

She gave a one shoulder shrug, amazed that he'd guessed correctly.

"Och, I am close. Ye wish to be the best archer in yer parents' eyes."

She shook her head and he arched a brow at her.

"Yer grandmother? Ye wished to impress yer grandmother more than yer parents?"

She didn't say anything but gave him the look that told him he was almost there. "Ye are close."

Brin pulled his head back. "Truly? I dinnae wish to say it. Ye must say it. I wish to hear this from yer verra lips, lass."

"All right. I wished to be the best in my grandsire's eyes." There she'd said it. It didn't matter what he thought because she couldn't change it. "Grandmama's too, if I am completely honest."

Brin nodded. "Ye are no' alone in that wish. Many people have tried to impress Logan Ramsay over the years. There were only a few who didnae care what he thought."

It was her turn to be shocked. "Who? I thought everyone cared what Grandsire thought. He was a spy with Grandmama, a favorite of our king."

"Uncle Alex didnae care. He was a legacy

in his own right, sword fighting. But the two were the best of friends, often seen chatting up on the parapets whenever they were together. Connor loves to talk about the two and their conversations. He said they'd argue until they'd find themselves chuckling over one event or another. And speaking of Connor, I think he was only interested in acting in his grandsire's eyes. He was strong-minded. Willing to risk falling in love with a lass of questionable reputation."

"I'll believe those two names, but no more. I know Jamie wished to be a great archer."

"True, but ye are forgetting one more. Yer Uncle Quade, God rest his soul. He didnae wish to be anything like his brother. They loved to argue, so I'm told. And they weren't left chuckling the way Uncle Alex and Logan were. They'd bellow loud enough to shake the rafters."

She laughed over that true comment, various memories of the two brothers arguing over many things, including Aunt Brenna.

He stood and moved over to the horse to give him the core of his apple, then reached out into a snowbank for a handful of snow to quench his thirst. "'Tis dark. The fire is waning and I wish to save the other dry wood. Mayhap we should try to get some sleep. Are ye tired enough to try?"

"Aye. I'm exhausted. Riding was strenuous and my leg continues to ache. I'll be able to sleep." Especially with Brin not far away.

The two fussed about, taking care of their own saddle bags, their own needs, before moving over to the back of the cave.

"At least the wind has slowed," Brin said. "And ye will sleep next to me. I'll no' take nay for an answer. Ye will need my heat."

Since she was already shivering, she did not argue with him. "I'll agree." How much colder would it get? She hated to find out. His heat would definitely be welcome, anything to stop the shaking that had overtaken her.

"I'll act honorably, I promise. I hope ye are no' worried."

The sincerity in his gaze struck her. He meant every word and she believed him. She said nothing, thinking on something entirely different. Her other regret. She still had her maidenhead and after all the tales she'd heard from her cousins, she wished she didn't.

He spread out two plaids across the stone to warm it, then settled, opening his arms to her. "Come. Put your back to me and I'll wrap my arms around ye to keep ye warm."

She did as he asked but said nothing.

"As I said, ye have my word that I'll act honorably."

She said nothing, settling against him, thrilled to feel his heat against her back, but thinking of exactly what she wished to say.

"What is it, lass? Are ye worried about something?"

She shook her head, but then whispered, "'Tis my other regret."

"What is it?"

"I still have my maidenhead but I wish I didnae. Mayhap 'tis a good time to give it away. I trust ye, Brin. I dinnae know if I will ever marry. And what if we dinnae survive? I wish to know what it feels like." There. She'd said exactly what was on her mind and held her breath, waiting for his response.

He turned her around to face him. "Ceit, as much as I am drawn to ye, I willnae take yer maidenhead without a priest or handfasting. I dinnae wish to have my bollocks cut off by yer sire nor shot off by yer grandmother. And yer grandsire? I fear what he would do…"

She couldn't stop herself from giggling. But then she became racked with shivers from the cold. "I dinnae know how long I can tolerate this cold, Brin. Even with ye beside me. I feel yer heat, but 'tis no' enough."

He reached for her mantle and began to unbutton it, doing the same with his own clothing. He unbuttoned and maneuvered until they were nearly skin to skin, just her short chemise separating them. Ceit blushed, but when she touched his chest, she couldn't stop the sigh of pleasure from leaving her lips. He grabbed the edge of both of their mantles and covered them completely, giving them plenty of room to cuddle beneath.

Finally, she warmed.

"Ceit, ye are a golden beauty." His lips touched hers lightly. "Am I too cold for ye?"

"Nay, ye are warm."

He kissed her, this time taking his time to explore her mouth, her tongue, even dragging the heat of his lips across her jawline and down her neck, her sighs of pleasure something she didn't try to hide. He kissed a trail to the valley between her breasts, then took one of her nipples in his mouth, laving her with such attention that she was nearly undone.

"Ceit, do ye trust me?"

"Aye. I do, Brin."

"I promise to show ye how good it can be between a husband and wife, but I vow no' to take yer maidenhead."

"'Tis possible?" She had no idea. The little she knew about lovemaking came from listening to Isla and Reyna talk about how wonderful it was, and the serving lasses' whispers about various deeds. But she'd reached the point that she wished to know.

All of it.

To know how it felt. What it meant.

"Aye, 'tis possible in many different ways. More than I can explain. 'Tis one of those things that is better shown in a demonstration. Just relax and trust me."

So she did.

Brin explored her body and caressed her in ways she'd never imagined, but she made up her mind not to be embarrassed about anything. To give herself over to his talented hands and lips. To enjoy herself. She closed her eyes and allowed his hands to roam, his caresses marvelous.

Every moment was wondrous.

At one point, she yelled out Brin's name as he brought her to a peak of enjoyment, some precipice that she needed to go over. Fall over it she did with a scream that left her panting. She clung to him, her breathing as fast as though she'd just been in battle.

The entire experience was sheer pleasure. And she'd had no idea such a thing was possible. "Brin, 'twas incredible. But ye…" She knew he'd not experienced the same finish she had.

"I am fine. And I have a wee bit more experience than ye, so worry no' about me, but I'm glad ye listened to me. Ye needed to trust me and I'm glad ye did. 'Twas only one way to enjoy each other's body."

She gasped and clung to Brin for his strength and his heat, leaning her head on his shoulder, taking in his scent, something special that only Brin could have created. Now that she was more aware of her surroundings, the cold was creeping inside her, grabbing hold of her very core.

"I pray we have the chance for me to learn more from ye, Brin."

She locked her gaze on his, and his worry was more than evident. The fire was gone, the snow continued to fall and they had little food left.

And they were losing their own heat quickly. "Brin, do ye think we will awaken in the morn? Have ye ever been in a situation like this?"

"Nay, I have no'. I've been hunting, and cold in those situations, times when I thought my fingers would fall off, but never overnight in a cave this cold, this isolated, without firewood."

He held her tight, giving her his heat and she thought it unfair. "Ye could survive possibly if I dinnae take all yer heat, would ye no'?"

"Nay. I'd not survive if I watched ye die because of my own selfishness. 'Tis no' me. I share what I have and gladly. Close yer eyes and go to sleep, lass. Fear no'. We will awaken and get across the ravine in the morn."

She let out a deep sigh. A cold deep sigh. But then another thought occurred to her.

If she died in Brin's arms, she'd die happy.

CHAPTER ELEVEN

B RIN AWAKENED AS the sun was dawning, casting that early morning eeriness into the cave, the cold gripping him hard. He stared at Ceit, her body so still that it frightened him. He couldn't stop himself from stirring her to make sure she was still alive. He'd wanted more from her, but he knew that to do so would steal all the strength from her core. He couldn't do it.

Her eyes opened slowly and he could see that though he'd barely pulled away from her, she'd already started shivering in the chill of the cave. He was feeling sluggish from the cold himself and knew he needed to get both of them up and moving quickly. What he would do for a bit more firewood.

He gave her a quick kiss and said, "I'll be right back, lass. Wrap up in the plaids until I return. I'll start the fire. We have a few pieces of dry wood left and we need them now."

Taking a moment to stretch once he stood, he swore he heard a noise outside the cave. The horses began to react, though fortunately not skittish at all. Perhaps they were as affected by the cold as he was, moving slowly. But the continued noise from outside was enough for him to move to the mouth of the cave. He silently prayed it wasn't a beast looking for shelter.

His timing was perfect.

A voice called out to him. "Help me! Brin, is that truly ye? God above has blessed us! Please help me get my wife inside."

The perilous snowstorm had ended, but it had left a white wonderland that glittered in the early morning sunlight, one too deep to battle yet.

He hurried out of the cave, tripping over fallen tree limbs heavily laden with snow, until he reached the man next to the horse, shocked to see it was indeed someone he knew.

"Padraig? What the hell are ye doing here? Did ye no' notice the storm? And Giselle is with ye?" A very pregnant Giselle, if he remembered correctly. It was hard to tell with a mantle hiding everything, but he didn't see a wee bairn anywhere so she had to still be with child.

Giselle was atop the horse, releasing a powerful screech of pain.

Padraig bellowed, "Dinnae ask questions now. She's about to have our bairn, and I swear she canno' have it on the horse. Help me get her inside. I'll explain our foolishness later."

Ceit stood in the mouth of the cave, fully dressed and wrapped in her mantle. "Giselle? 'Tis truly ye on that horse?"

Brin helped Giselle down while Padraig grabbed his saddle bag with his free hand, his other hand still on his wife, unwilling to let her go. He glanced at Giselle's face, now grimacing and writhing in pain, then at Padraig, his face deeply etched with worry.

"Our bairn. We'll have to help her deliver the bairn in the cave. I prayed we could make it here first, but I fear we made a big mistake leaving Cameron land."

"I made ye, so stop fussing," Giselle hissed. "Just get this screamin' bairn out of me."

Brin decided to keep his comments to himself. After watching Giselle nearly fall in the snow, tripping over a hidden tree root, he scooped her up and carried her inside, past the horses and into the quiet of the back of the cave.

"Mighty cold to deliver a bairn, Padraig." He looked to his friend to see what his response would be.

"Do I look like I care that the cave is cold?" The worry on his friend's face told Brin much. Padraig had been traveling alone with a woman about to deliver her bairn in the middle of a snowstorm. His usual calm exterior was anything but at the moment, his eyes wide and his jaw tense. "I have two bags of warm plaids and blankets from yer dear mother. She made me carry them and now I know why. And why is there no fire in here?"

"I'll get right to it, but we are low on wood. We used the stack last eve when we were forced to find cover from the brutal storm. Mayhap I can go look for dry wood, somewhere. Did ye see any protected area where the snow didn't hit? If so, I'd gladly get the wood. Take a horse if I must."

He looked to his friend for some insight since Padraig and Giselle traveled this area often.

Padraig handed Ceit the saddle bags and the two did their best to create a bed for poor Giselle while she paced and cursed. "Dammit all to hell but this hurts. This is the only one, Padraig. Never again."

Padraig said, "Aye, lass. No more bairns for us. I agree!" He said it a wee bit too enthusiastically.

"Arghhh," Giselle yelled, grabbing her midsection as if it could stop her pain.

Ceit took her hand and talked to her calmly, though Brin didn't miss how Ceit's hands shook from the cold.

The fire. I must start the fire.

He busied himself arranging the last bits of dry wood they had while Padraig walked outside and returned, dumping a huge pile of dry wood in the back of the cave. "Why have ye no' used this yet?"

Astounded by the amount of wood in front of him, he asked, "Where the hell did ye find it? All the wood I could find is wet from the heavy snow."

"From my stash."

"Yer stash?"

"Aye, my stash. I travel often if ye have no' noticed, Brin. So I make sure we always leave enough dry wood for the next ones." His voice increased in volume and speed. "Do ye think I am an idjit or something?"

"Ahhhhh…." Another screech came from Giselle and Padraig's eyes widened.

Brin stopped his cousin's movement, clasping his shoulder. "Padraig, we'll help ye. The two of ye arenae alone. I've seen my mother deliver many babes under different situations. Ceit can certainly help. Calm yerself. I'll build the fire so we can make sure the bairn is warm. 'Tis important." He had to admit the situation did make him a wee bit concerned, the evidence in his own rambling short sentences. His mother's words echoed in his mind. *Ye must keep a newly born bairn warm. 'Tis most important.* Which is exactly why she sent along the extra plaids.

Padraig sighed and then hugged Brin. "Ye have no idea how glad I was to see ye come out of that cave. We hoped to be ahead of the storm, just get to the coast where the snow wouldn't be. Giselle wished to deliver our bairn at Eddirdale Castle in Brigid's capable hands, surrounded by her brothers, but 'tis no' to be. We had no idea this storm would march on through at this time of year."

"Naught about this bairn is to be expected, Padraig. I'm too old, it's too cold. We're too late. Nay, too early. Too much snow. Lord above, please help us," Giselle moaned out the last phrase, clutching her belly at the same time. "I fear it willnae be long!"

"We'll promise to help ye get the bairn so Aunt Brigid can see her within her first few days of life. I'll start the fire. Ceit will get a place settled for Giselle to deliver the bairn, and ye comfort yer wife."

"Ye canno' comfort a woman with pains like

this, Brin." He made a point to ignore Padraig's narrowed gaze locked on him.

"Aye, ye can. 'Tis yer job, Padraig." Brin decided to do what his mother had done many times, take charge and dole out tasks that needed to be done. "Ceit, we'll need water. Fill the skins on all the horses. Once ye warm yerself by the fire, ye'll take our daggers out to clean them, and we'll also need some clean linen strips." He brought Ceit close and hugged her, kissing her forehead. "I know ye are cold, but ye'll warm soon."

Ceit rubbed her hands together. "I'm warming already."

Giselle's voice came out in a shrill question as she reached for her husband. "Why do ye need a dagger? I changed my mind, Padraig. I'm not going to have this bairn. I'm going to keep it inside forever." Giselle looked at him, then placed her forehead against his chest, whimpering as another contraction took control.

Padraig looked at Brin and mouthed the word, "Daggers?"

Brin said, "We have to cut the cord and cut linen strips too." He built his wood pile and worked on lighting it, saving some for later. He knew one thing from being around his mother. One never knew how long it would take Giselle to deliver this wee one. It could be an hour or a day. One could never be certain.

"Ye've done this before, Brin?" Giselle asked, her gaze hopeful. "I mean, the details. The stuff that comes out after. The cord. The bairn. Ye know what I mean."

"Not on my own, but I've assisted Mama several times. Bairns like to come in the middle of the night and once Tara and Riley disappeared, she often grabbed me to go along with her. I helped with supplies mostly, but I watched enough to help ye. Ye'll not stop the wee thing once it has decided it wishes to meet ye."

Ceit asked, "Do ye wish for a laddie or lassie?"

Brin gave her a nod of encouragement, approving of her method of distracting Giselle.

Giselle replied, "I care no'."

"Have ye chosen yer names yet?" Ceit continued as she saw to her tasks.

"Bairn," Giselle announced. "Wee bairn."

Padraig said, "Nay, Giselle. I thought a nice name would be Mud or mayhap Coo for a lass."

"We're no' naming our bairn after a coo, Padraig."

"Then Sheepy. Or Horsey. Or Dirty."

Giselle slapped his arm playfully, but she did smile. "Stop yer tales." Then her eyes filled with tears. "But I dinnae know what we will name a wee lassie."

"We'll think of something. We'll wait to see what we have first. No sense spending time on a lassie's name if ye plan to give me a son." Padraig held her close and rubbed her back.

Brin came over to Ceit and motioned for her to follow him to the other side of the flames that were now building from the new wood Padraig had found them. "Warm yerself, lass. I'll need yer help for this. Have ye seen a bairn birthed before?"

She shook her head. "I've heard much talk. But I've no' watched. Ye will have to tell me what to do."

"I'll do the tough work. The hardest part is catching the wee bairn when she pushes it out. 'Tis a slippery thing."

Ceit paled, so he kissed her forehead. "Trust me, 'tis a most humbling event when 'tis over. Ye'll see. Dinnae be frightened by Giselle. 'Tis most painful, but also extremely rewarding."

He did his best not to let on how nervous he was about the upcoming birth. He'd observed many times, but never done it himself. If there were any problems, he didn't know what he would do.

Brin wiped the sweat from his brow and moved over to speak with Padraig. "Are ye ready?"

"Hell, but I thought ye'd never say so, Brin. Deliver our bairn, will ye no'?"

"Giselle, just tell me how ye'll be most comfortable," he said as calmly as he could.

"How the hell would I know? I've never done this before. I've only heard all the screaming from Brigid's chamber."

After much thought he said, "The stone surface will be too hard for ye. Padraig, ye sit here and lean yer back against the wall, and she can sit in front of ye. Between yer legs so ye can help support her back. She'll need it for certes."

The two positioned themselves as he suggested. Then Brin kneeled in front of them, settling himself. It wasn't long before Giselle let out a scream.

"Here it comes! Please, Brin. Catch this bairn. Get it out!"

Brin motioned for Ceit to sit next to him, then did the only other thing he knew how to do for certain.

He prayed.

CHAPTER TWELVE

CEIT HAD HEARD many comments about childbirth, but she'd never expected it to proceed the way it did. Messy, loud, difficult, slow, undignified. What other words would fit?

At one point, Giselle finished one push, resting back against her husband and shouted, "Ceit, never ever have a bairn. Do what ye must to prevent it. This will kill me for certes."

Ceit didn't know how to react to that, but felt it deserved a response. "I hadn't any plans to have bairns. I'll tell my parents. Cadyn can make them grandparents, not me."

"If yer smart, ye'll never marry." The last word came out in a screech as Giselle propelled herself forward for another push.

Padraig said, "Dinnae tell her that, love. She deserves to have her bairns."

"Then dinnae wait too long. I'm too old to do this. I'm over forty, if ye must know. Have them now."

Ceit had no idea what had transpired in their marriage. She knew the two had traveled to care for any young children who were sick. Padraig had considered becoming a physician just for bairns, but he hadn't trained officially. The two only did their work from experience and by talking with the experts they met along the way.

"And this is yer first?" she asked innocently. By the way Brin's eyes widened, she guessed it was a sensitive question.

Padraig replied, "We had hoped to have many bairns, but it was no' to be. Just when we gave up hope, Giselle found herself carrying. We had her checked by a midwife in London and she confirmed our suspicions. She advised she could have trouble carrying the bairn to the end because of her advanced years…"

"I wish she were here to call me advanced years now," Giselle roared. "I'll tell her a thing or two. Och, another one, Padraig. Help me push."

Padraig supported her back by pushing himself forward and the force continued until the poor woman was red in the face and gasping for air.

Ceit had never seen anything like it. She mopped Giselle's brow with a cool linen cloth, but then moved as the hard-working mother collapsed against her husband.

"Almost there, Giselle. I can see the hair on its head," Brin said. "Mayhap the next push or two will do it."

"I canno' do any more," she said, tears filling her eyes. "Padraig will have to deliver this bairn. Ye must push, husband. I'm leaving. I'm going out the cave and not coming back until the bairn is lying in yer arms." Tear flooded her cheeks but she didn't move.

No one said anything, allowing the poor woman to ramble on. Ceit decided to look at the ceiling in the cave, ignoring the unfortunate woman's frustration. The poor thing had to be exhausted.

With a sudden roar, Giselle forced herself back to a sitting position and pushed again, and with one more bellow, the bairn slipped out of its home into Brin's capable hands.

"A lad? A lassie?" Padraig asked, squeezing Giselles's shoulders in front of him, then wrapping his arms around her when she settled against him. "Ye did it, lass. And a fine job."

Brin wiped the bairn's face just as she broke into a husky cry, a sound that made each of them smile. "A lass! Congratulations on your new daughter!"

Giselle broke into sobs, and Ceit had to pinch herself to move. The entire episode had frightened the hell out of her until this moment. She peered down at the new bairn in Brin's capable hands, astonished at how the breath of life had changed this into a wondrous occasion.

She understood. Unfolding the plaid, she wished to warm the babe quickly.

Brin handed the bairn to her. "Hold on to this wee one while I tie off the cord. Then ye can clean her up properly while I tend to Giselle's new contractions."

"What the hell is this?" Giselle bellowed as she bent forward again. "No' another? Please, nay!"

"Nay, 'tis the part that feeds the bairn. Ye have

no need of it anymore so yer body will expel it. Once we rid ye of that and cut the cord, Ceit will hand the bairn to ye so ye can put her to yer breast. Ceit, once the cord is cut, take the bairn closer to the fire and clean her up with the linen strips, then wrap her in a clean, warm blanket."

Ceit did as she was instructed, hanging on to the wee lass tightly as she cleaned her off. The lass still cried a bit, but once she was wrapped in the clean plaid, she stared up at Ceit.

Ceit was transfixed.

"May I hold her, please?" Giselle asked.

Ceit shook her head slightly to jar herself. "Of course. Here she is."

Giselle looked at Padraig. "Is she not lovely?"

"Aye," he agreed, his hand coming up under Giselle's to help support the wee one. Ceit noticed Giselle had fine tremors, but her husband knew exactly what to do. "Try to feed her. Put her right to yer breast. We've seen it many times. The best thing for our bairn."

Brin said, "He's right, Giselle. I've heard Mama say the same. Try to nurse her. Ye'll give her yer warmth too."

Padraig said, "Tease her mouth with yer nipple."

Ceit watched the event, fascinated as the wee babe searched for her mother and finally suckled, taking a moment or two to latch on tightly, but she did. The bairn calmed instantly, her eyes locked on her mother, her tiny fists clenched while her father looked over Giselle's shoulder.

If only she could freeze that image for the couple. It was one of the most beautiful sights she'd ever seen. The most beautiful event she'd ever participated in.

Brin said, "Ceit, would ye help me over here, please?"

She moved to his side and helped him finish up with Giselle, cleaning her the best they could before wrapping her tight in two more plaids. "Good thing my mother sent all the extra plaids along."

A bellow caught them all by surprise. "Cameron, are ye still here? I see horses outside, but they are no' yers."

Maitland stepped into the mouth of the cave. "Och, here are yer beasts. Then whose are outside?" He moved around the two animals, giving them each a push to move outside. "The weather is clearing. Get out there." He smiled once they moved out, only to freeze as he took in the sight in front of him. "Am I seeing a bairn in front of me or did I hit my head?"

Brin stepped away after washing his hands in a pile of snow that had blown in. "Ye are seeing a bairn. Padraig and Giselle decided they wished to beat the storm so they could make it to Black Isle before it hit. Didn't work verra well for them."

Padraig stepped away from his wife, who was still nursing their newly born daughter. "Aye, thank the Lord that Brin and Ceit were here. I was in a panic thinking it was entirely on my shoulders delivering the bairn. Many thanks to ye, Brin." Then he called over his shoulder, "And to ye, Ceit." She was still helping Giselle to get settled again.

Ceit nodded but couldn't help but wonder how they would get such a small bairn home safely in the cold.

Maitland said, "Ye are in luck that I did what I did."

Brin gave him a puzzled look.

"I brought a cart in case either of ye were injured. 'Tis on the far side of the ravine. If we can get Giselle to there, she'll ride more comfortably with the wee one wrapped up tightly."

That comment brought understanding to Ceit. Thinking of all Giselle had just been through, riding a horse would not be a simple task. "And what about the bairn?" she asked the two men, noticing that Giselle had closed her eyes while the baby suckled. "Will that no' be too cold for her in the cart?"

Padraig said, "The wee lass will travel against my chest. 'Twas Aunt Maddie who said the wee ones were always happiest sleeping against a man's chest. Uncle Alex strapped all their bairns to his chest, even when he was in the lists. We're warmer."

Brin said, "When should we plan on leaving?"

Maitland said, "Right away. We'll do what we can for Giselle, but another storm is on the horizon, and the ravine may not be passable after another day. Besides, we could use yer help at Eddirdale Castle. We have a few injuries to tend to."

"Who is hurt?" Ceit asked, saying a quick prayer.

"Ysenda and Lewis. They'll not be leaving

Black Isle for a while. And there were several Matheson guards injured in a boar attack. Jennet and Tara are overwhelmed. And they'll be even more pleased to hear Padraig is here."

Giselle looked at her husband and said, "Come, Padraig. Let us take wee Caralyn home with us."

Maitland said, "A most fitting name after yer mother, Padraig. Caralyn was a fine woman and healer."

Padraig hurried back, kissed his wife, and lifted his new daughter. "Greetings, wee Lynie. I love ye so much already."

One horse let out a noise none of them liked.

Maitland and Brin ran to the mouth of the cave, then Brin turned back. "Giselle, we have to ready ye for travel."

"So soon?" she asked, looking exhausted.

Maitland said, "'Tis yer only chance to make it through the ravine. The snow has started up again. We leave now or ye head back to Grant land."

"Black Isle, here we come!"

CHAPTER THIRTEEN

B RIN DIDN'T HAVE a chance to chat with
Ceit much on the way to Matheson land.
They passed through the ravine as slowly as
possible for Giselle's sake, but as soon as they
made it through, she breathed a sigh of relief for
all of them.

Padraig had the baby strapped to his chest
under his mantle, and the baby slept happily for
most of the time. She didn't need to be fed until
they were past the snowstorm and near the coast
of the firth, the water keeping the snow at bay.

They stopped long enough for Giselle to feed
wee Lynie, as she was already being called by
both parents, and the rest ate their meager supply
of oatcakes and dried meat.

They arrived at Eddirdale Castle just before the
evening meal, and they were greeted excitedly,
especially by the new aunts and uncles to wee
Caralyn.

Brin had barely finished a trencher of pottage
inside when he was called by his sister into the
healing chamber. "Brin, we could use yer help.
We had four guards attacked by boars who need

their dressings changed. It really takes two hands. Ceit has volunteered to tend the first one in the back. Would ye mind helping her?"

"Not at all, I'd be happy to assist in any way possible. Where are they?"

"We'll send them in one at a time. Lewis took a hard fall down the ravine, so he is in the one bed in the chamber. Ysenda also broke a bone in her leg, so she is sleeping here also. We just straightened her bone, and she is in a great deal of pain. Jennet and I are working with them. Riley is not feeling well so that leaves Ceit and ye. Ye have the experience the others lack."

"Aye. Where is the poultice and the linen strips?"

Tara pointed to a bed in the corner. "Ceit has started but 'tis too large a wound for her. She needs another set of hands." Then she whispered, "Besides, she is awfully cute."

Brin rolled his eyes and walked away, but not before whispering between gritted teeth, "Ye sound like Papa. Please dinnae."

He ignored Tara's giggle and marched to the back of the large chamber to where Ceit sat on a stool next to a table covered with linen strips, a basin of water, and a jar of poultice. She started when he scraped a stool across the floor to join her. "I can help. I hear this guard has a large wound."

"Aye, Timm is struggling with the pain so I'd like to be quick with it. I was just about to start removing the linen strips, but he said it hurts to pull on them. Ye could help me, and we could make quick work of it."

"Hurts badly, Timm?"

Timm nodded, his white fists at his sides telling Brin all he needed to know.

"We can fix that." Brin moved over to the cabinet with the healer potions and returned with a small goblet. "Here, Timm. Drink this. We'll be done sooner."

Timm gave him an odd look but took the goblet gratefully and drank it, falling asleep shortly after he set the goblet down. Brin looked at Ceit's surprised face and said, "Mama never believed in making patients sit through the pain. Tara uses the same potion Mama did. He'll awaken in an hour or two feeling refreshed, no memory of this."

Ceit nodded, then said, "I'm not sure what I'm doing exactly. Can ye help? Tara told me to clean the wound, apply the poultice, then put clean linen strips and tie them so they will stay on. I understand about keeping things clean as my aunt Brenna insisted on cleaning our hands. I'm sure I'm able to complete the last two parts about the poultice and the linen, but what does she mean by clean the wound?"

Brin said, "Och, we can do that in no time. I'll show ye." He reached for the basin filled with water, a small cup next to it. "I'm sure we were both trained the same as my mother often told me that she believed in everything that Aunt Brenna did. My mother worked with her for many years."

"Aye, so ye understand keeping things clean.

A woman I met didnae understand the concept, which I thought odd, but we were raised that way. Agree?"

"True. My mother used to make us wash our hands before we handled food. Everyone thought she was daft but I did it because she said we'd be stronger for it. Who knows if she is correct in her beliefs? I decided it was easier to do as she asked than to upset her by ignoring her wishes."

Ceit giggled. "I always believed the same, but Jennet didnae. They say she always argued with her mother."

"And now she is a wonderful healer too."

"It seems 'tis so much to learn about healing. What is the cup for?" Ceit asked.

"Ye'll see." He removed the linen strip as carefully as he could, pulling on a few spots where the threads of the linen stuck to the wound. It was still raw and a wee bit bloody, but there was evidence of green pus in one area, white in the other. "This green part we wish to wash away. It's the part that lets the healer know that there could be fever coming. 'Tis a sign of infection, and we dinnae wish for that to happen."

"Infection? Ye mean fever?"

"In a way. Infection means something is poisoning the wound. 'Tis the reason we put the poultice on. To try to kill the poison. Once I listened to the two discuss where the poison came from. It was a most interesting conversation."

"Where does it come from?"

"They dinnae know for sure. Aunt Brenna thought from something in the air. My mother thought it came from inside a person, from their blood. Aunt Brenna said she talked to someone who said it comes from the water. Just like the curse. It was all about the four humors or something like that. I didnae understand it."

Ceit dipped her head close to the wound, peering at the thick green fluid in the center of his wound. "It smells odd."

Brin nodded. "Verra astute of ye. Ye are a wise one, Ceit MacAdam." His gaze locked on hers, and he had a sudden memory of the two of them together in the cave. Of how sweet her lips had tasted.

How magnificent she'd been when he'd helped her find her pleasure. Magnificent and lovely.

She blushed at his momentary stare. "Is something wrong?"

"Nay, I just have pleasant memories of us." He smiled and then returned to his work. "We better finish before Timm awakens." Getting his supplies all together, he continued, "Smell is one of the ways my mother can tell if a wound is poisoned badly. 'Tis no' just the appearance, but how it feels to the person. She looks at the colors because they are verra important."

"What color is the worst?" she asked.

"Green. When it turns white, she thinks the poultice is working, but if it goes yellow or green, that is bad. So we need to clean it or wipe the green away before applying the poultice."

"How do we do that? With the cloth?"

"If 'tis a small area, I just wipe it. If it's larger, like this one, I pour water over it. That seems to loosen it a wee bit, makes it easier to wipe away."

They worked together, Brin explaining what he did along the way. It was indeed easier to change the linen with another set of hands, so they proceeded quickly, cleaning the wound, applying the poultice with a focus on the green area, then wrapping the leg with clean linen strips.

And all the while, Brin had trouble focusing on their task instead of the beautiful lass next to him. Ceit was beautiful, her golden hair much like her mother's hair, and she had the perfect lips for kissing—not too plump, not too thin. Pleasingly pink. Now he knew all her other attributes, and that made it more difficult than ever.

He knew how her breasts felt in his hands, he knew the taste of her skin, the arch of her back, even how quickly her nipples peaked from his touch.

Ceit was an intriguing woman. More talented than most, she had a skill in archery that few had and a tenacity to battle that many men didn't have. But sitting next to her in the healing chamber taught him something else. She had a bright mind, the kind his mother had often remarked about.

Ceit was curious. Her questions about healing were frequent and illustrated an understanding of the process much quicker than others he'd seen at the task, even his sisters. His mother would have to repeat herself when teaching them, but not Ceit. She absorbed the new information like she'd been thirsting for this knowledge all her life.

Hell, but he was falling for Ceit MacAdam.

CHAPTER FOURTEEN

CEIT HAD NEVER been more uncertain about anything or anyone than Brin Cameron. Being so close to him totally unsettled her, even if it was simply sitting near him in a healing chamber. In fact, she was so overpowered by his scent that she dropped her head to take in the pungent odor of Timm's wound to distract herself from this gorgeous man now sitting so close to her that she wished to lean over and nibble his strong jawline.

His eyes appeared more blue than she'd ever seen them, so mesmerizing that she had to pull her gaze away to focus on the wound, or he'd be wondering what was wrong with her. She fought the memory of their time together from dominating her mind at the moment.

She couldn't allow it. It had been too embarrassing. But she'd also believed they'd never make it out of that cave together. In fact, the only reason she had survived was probably because of Brin's heat and then the arrival of Padraig and Giselle. The extra wood had saved her from a cold death, she was certain.

Brin explained, "Now that we have the wound cleaned, we can apply poultice like this."

Watching his hands work on that wound brought her mind back to the soft, gentle strokes he'd used on her not long ago, but they'd become hard as he'd brought her to that peak of pleasure she'd never experienced before.

"What?" he asked, wiping the poultice from his hand before tying the first linen strip around Timm's lower leg.

"I was just thinking…"

He tied one more strip around the wound, then sat back. "Ceit, we should probably talk about it. I know what ye are thinking about, the same as I am. But remember that we didnae know if we would ever make it out of that cave." He paused and looked at her, his hands reaching out for her but then dropping as he looked around him. "I should no' have done what I did. It was wrong of me to assume ye wanted me to…"

"But I did want ye to do… I just…I'm so embarrassed. I…I…" She didn't have any idea how to express exactly how she was feeling.

Like she could be falling in love with Brin for so many reasons beyond his fine looks. He was a patient, kind man with nimble fingers. His touch had been gentle, was gentle with Timm. He wasn't harsh and brusque and bossy and so many other things she was used to seeing in the men in her clan. There was a softness to him that excited her, but yet he was still more than capable of yielding a sword or a bow.

Considerate. That was the word she wished to

use. Nay. Compassionate. She didn't know men could be so compassionate and considerate.

Not at all like her sire and grandsire.

She blushed and he reached for her hand, clasping it inside both of his. "Dinnae be embarrassed. 'Twas a beautiful thing. I…"

Uncle Marcas appeared out of nowhere next to them and neither noticed until it was too late to break apart. True, they were only touching with their hands, but Ceit still blushed under her uncle's perusal. She didn't know Uncle Marcas as well as her Aunt Brigid, obviously, but she thought him a reasonable man.

"Ceit, is there something I should know about what transpired along the journey here?"

Her uncle's fists settled on his hips as his penetrating gaze caught her off guard.

"I dinnae know what ye mean, Uncle."

"The two of ye were in the cave together before Padraig appeared. Alone, I've just learned."

Tara appeared next to her uncle. "Marcas, what is going on? Why are ye questioning them?"

Uncle Marcas turned to Brin's sister and explained, "I'm just asking a question since I learned that Ceit and Brin were in the cave alone overnight. Padraig did not arrive until the next day and Maitland's group was on the other side of the ravine. I wish to know if my niece has been compromised."

Brin's eyes widened as he stood, dropping Ceit's hands. "Nay, Marcas. I can assure ye Ceit still has her maidenhead. We tried to stay alive and we managed. Naught more."

Uncle Marcas's brow arched. "Ceit. Is this true?"

"Aye," she replied, hopping out of her chair. "Why are ye questioning us as if we are criminals? We lived through an avalanche, a brutal snowstorm, and helped deliver Giselle's bairn. Should ye no' be thanking us?"

Suddenly annoyed more than she'd ever been with anyone, she bolted from her stool and crossed her arms. "Are ye accusing me of something?"

"Nay, I'm asking Brin if he acted honorably under the circumstances."

"Of course," the two replied in unison.

Uncle Marcas glanced from one to the other, then said, "Ceit, I think we should talk privately with yer Aunt Brigid."

Tara said, "And I'd like to speak with Brin privately too. Come, we'll find Shaw, Riley, and Torcall. I dinnae like how this is going." She gave Marcas a glaring look and then whirled around to head to the door, speaking to one of her assistants before leaving.

Brin gave her a small nod before turning to take his leave, but he was stopped in the doorway by Riley. "What is going on, Brin?"

Aunt Brigid came in behind Riley. "Marcas? What is happening? I heard rumblings in the hall that I didnae like."

"Truly, Uncle Marcas? Must ye embarrass me so?" Ceit asked the question, but she really wished to make haste and run out the door rather than be subjected to such a ridiculous inquisition. She stayed because Brin was still there too.

"I'm sorry if ye think I am embarrassing ye,

Ceit, but these questions must be asked. I would no' be doing my job as part of Brigid's family if I dinnae." Uncle Marcas pursed his lips and stood in the middle of the now large group. "Brigid, I'm here to protect yer niece. Someone needs to. She was stuck in the snowstorm alone with Brin."

"So what does that mean?" Riley asked, her eyes darkening. "I'm sure they were just trying to stay alive."

Then the worst happened, and Ceit regretted staying to hear the rest of the conversation. She should have taken her leave.

Uncle Marcas said, "Should there be a wedding soon between Ceit and Brin?"

Ceit shouted, "Nay!" at the same exact moment as Brin's bellow carried across the chamber.

"Nay!" Brin repeated. "Naught happened. There is no need for a wedding. Ask Ceit. She'll tell ye the truth." Brin turned to Ceit and the fury in his eyes caught her completely off guard. So she did the only thing she could think of.

She ran out the door.

CHAPTER FIFTEEN

TARA SAID, "WE will discuss this with Brin. Brigid, ye speak with Ceit and please tell yer husband to calm down before we meet again to discuss this."

Brigid nodded. "Agreed." Then she cast a murderous look at her husband before she spun around and followed Ceit. Over her shoulder, she growled, "Marcas?"

Brin was relieved to see them go. He hadn't meant to yell so at Ceit. He'd have to apologize later, but they had riled his temper, something that didn't happen often.

Riley said, "I'd prefer to find Torcall and discuss this privately, Tara. Where is Shaw and where shall we meet?"

Tara glanced around and said, "All three patients are sound asleep. Go find Shaw and Torcall and bring them here. I dinnae wish to be overheard by all the servants."

Brin paced, but he didn't have to wait long. Shaw barreled through the door a few moments later, Riley and Torcall behind him. "What the hell is going on? Everyone is up in arms, and the whole clan is discussing our problems. I dinnae like that. What is this about, Tara?"

Brin said, "May I please explain, sister?"

"Of course," Tara motioned for the five of them to sit at the table near the front of the chamber.

Brin took a stool and said, "We were traveling under the instructions of our king to chase an English garrison that was supposed to be near Inverness. We learned of the impending snowstorm so decided to push through the ravine first, figuring if we made it to the other side that we could either come here or head to Inverness depending on the weather."

Shaw said, "Wise thinking. Bound to be heavy snow this early in the season, and once ye made it through the coast is not far. Whose idea?"

"Dyna and Maitland made that decision together. We were nearly to the ravine when the snow became heavy and swirling, but we made the attempt to cross in the snow. Ceit was ahead of me at the back of the line, Maitland ahead of her. There was an avalanche, as ye probably know, and we were the only two at the rear."

Tara added, "Had ye been in front of Maitland, ye would have been sent over the edge by the avalanche, just as Ysenda and Lewis were. They'll both survive but 'twas no' easy getting them here with their injuries. But go on."

Brin took a deep breath and said, "It was nearly dark. Once the avalanche ended, we heard Maitland's bird call, asking how we were. He advised us to wait for the storm to end before attempting passage. And they moved on."

Shaw said, "There was no other possibility. If the heavy snow had already taken two down and made the ravine impassable, ye had no choice but to stay behind. Ye were not far from the Grant cave so ye stayed there, aye?"

"We considered trying to make it to Grant land, but dark was upon us and the snow continued, that swirling mesmerizing snow I hate. So we stayed in the Grant cave where we could keep the horses safe and where we knew there would be dry wood for a fire."

"And if ye'd gone on, ye both would have been found dead in the snow. Ye made the only decision ye could. What is my brother's issue?" Shaw asked.

Tara said, "He's playing the concerned uncle and asking Ceit if she was compromised."

"Hellfire." Shaw stood so quickly he knocked over his stool. "Marcas is playing laird so I'll go talk with him. Did he try to suggest marriage? Because those are all the words on the servants' mouths. They all think there'll be a big wedding on the morrow."

The door opened and Ethan stepped in. "I have come as an unbiased person." Jennet crept in behind him.

She said, "I'm to keep quiet. I'm just here to listen." She gave a side grin and waggled her brow at the group.

"Go ahead, Ethan," Shaw said. "What did they send ye here to do?"

"I have specific instructions, if ye dinnae mind."

They all knew that Ethan would do as instructed so Shaw said, "Go ahead. Ask yer questions and if we need more discussion we'll send ye away for a bit."

"Agreed," Ethan said, his one arm loosely wrapped around Jennet's shoulders. "Brin, did ye compromise Ceit in any way?"

"Nay, I did no'." He didn't hesitate to answer. Showing her the glory of her body did not compromise her in any way for her future husband. He was being truthful.

"Brin, did ye take Ceit's maidenhead?"

"Nay!" This time he stood and Shaw clasped his shoulder but he shrugged him away, glaring at Ethan. "I dinnae like this. How many different ways do ye need to ask me?"

Ethan said, "I only have one more question for ye, then one for the group."

Brin said, "Go ahead."

"Did ye kiss Ceit at all?"

"'Tis none of yer business, Ethan. And tell Marcas 'tis not his concern either. We are both adults."

Tara and Riley stood and applauded their brother.

Ysenda shouted from her bed in the back, "'Tis about time ye did, Brin Cameron."

Then Tara said, "Mayhap Brin was compromised. Did ye no' think on that, Ethan?" Brin laughed at that. His sisters were both always fighting the male way of the world.

Jennet muttered, "Since Brin is twice Ceit's age, I doubt that, though 'twas a fair question." She giggled then covered her mouth. "Continue with yer last question, Ethan."

"To the group, do ye wish fer any restitution for what happened between Brin and Ceit?"

Five voices shouted, "Nay!"

Brin sat down again with a sigh as Ethan and Jennet took their leave.

Shaw said, "Brin, because she is family, ye may have to do the right thing. Are ye prepared for that? Have ye considered who her sire and grandsire are?"

Brin ran his hand down his face with frustration. "I…what…I…" Hellfire, but he didn't like other people telling him what to do. "Nay, I did naught wrong. They canno' tell me what to do!"

Riley reached for his hand and squeezed it. "Brin, the situation could be worse. I think ye and Ceit make a nice couple, and it would put an end to Papa's persistent push to marry ye off."

Brin looked at his sister, a pair of green eyes in his mind. "I know that, but do ye no' think that if we were to marry that it would be best if we did it on our own terms?"

Riley tilted her head and said, "True."

Tara whispered, "Brother, stop being so stubborn. Ye have feelings for her. Just marry her."

Brin got up and strolled out the door, heading to the back entrance. He had to get the hell away. And he had no idea where he was going.

His sisters were correct. If he were forced to marry anyone, Ceit would be the best choice. He definitely had feelings for her, though it was not the love he'd hoped to have long ago. But he could see a good life with Ceit, perhaps they would come to love one another.

But he wished for this decision to be on their terms, not forced because of an unwarranted storm. It would not bode well for either of them to be forced into marriage. He'd heard her outcries as much as his own.

He'd rather have the chance to pursue the lass on his own terms.

He wasn't budging on that.

CHAPTER SIXTEEN

CEIT HEADED UP the staircase to her chamber. She didn't wish to speak to anyone at this point.

Least of all Brin.

The look on his face when someone suggested marriage made every feeling she'd had for him disintegrate into a swirl of dark snow flurries. She hated this entire situation.

Hated what they'd done. Hated the snow, the avalanche, everyone at this point.

Even Brin. She wished to go home.

She closed the door behind her and threw herself onto her bed, willing the tears to stay away for a wee bit more. How she wished she were home in her own bedchamber on Ramsay land. With people she could discuss freely and ask questions, especially due to this uncommon situation. If she were to guess, she'd be discussing this soon. Someone would follow her so she'd have to save her tears for later.

Aunt Brigid's quiet knock interrupted her thoughts. "May I come in, Ceit?"

She sighed and said, "Enter."

Aunt Brigid came in and sat on the end of the bed. "May we chat?"

"Aye, but I have little to say." She wasn't going to tell anyone what truly happened between them. She was too embarrassed, and the entire night had naught to do with her maidenhead.

"May I speak? And if I do so, will you listen?" Aunt Brigid asked. She smoothed the fine fabric of her dress. Her aunt was still a beautiful woman, her chestnut-colored hair in waves down her back with a few strands of gray. She was more careful about her appearance than their cousin, Jennet, but she had her own way to flaunt the usual conventions for women. She refused to plait her hair every day.

Jennet refused to wear gowns and dressed in leggings unless it was a special event. The two had numerous tales about the trouble they often found themselves in during their younger days, including the time King Alexander favored them because of Jennet's clever way of saving Torrian from a forced marriage.

She scowled, recalling that even that story was about chicken blood and a lass's maidenhead.

Ceit muttered, "I will listen, but it is revolting the way women are judged so quickly. I was on patrol, and if every time a lass goes on patrol and gets stuck with a man, the reaction is to force a wedding, you'll have a hard time finding any man who will agree to go on patrol or even battle with a woman."

Aunt Brigid tipped her head, thought for a moment, and said, "I agree with ye. I dinnae think ye will be forced to marry Brin. So please dinnae ask. But I'll offer this as a reason while we are asking questions. If yer sire or grandsire were here, would they ask any questions?"

"I dinnae want either of them here." She grabbed a pillow and covered her face. "Go ahead and I'll listen."

"I'm unsure whether or no' ye have heard the tale of Torrian and Heather, but Heather doesn't hesitate to tell the tale of how she was taken advantage of by a verra wealthy nobleman."

Ceit sat up, interested in this tale that she'd never heard about the chieftain's wife. "I've no' heard this. Please go on, Aunt Brigid."

"Heather lived with her grandparents and was often in the forest. A man came along and showered her with gifts. I will no' go into the details, but he eventually managed to get her with child and she didnae even know it had happened. She was too young to understand and he took advantage of her. She states that she didn't even realize what he was about until it was too late. Not having her mother around to discuss these types of things with made it difficult for her. She had no idea how bairns were made and didn't ask questions until her belly began to grow."

Ceit thought about this and wondered how she could not know, but then wondered if Brin had tried the same, would she have known? She knew that at one point, she would have allowed him to do anything to her, anything to get over that precipice. Had Heather experienced something similar? "Is that who fathered Nellie?"

Aunt Brigid nodded. "Heather was younger than ye are, but I tell ye this because most lasses are rather naïve about the entire situation. Marcas tells me men talk about it all the time, but I can tell ye that women rarely talk about the true event. They talk around it. The way the servants talk about teasing a man and having their pleasure. All things that never say exactly what happens. Having lived among healers does make ye more aware of the situation, but I'm here to ask ye if ye have any questions for me. I know no' what yer mother has discussed with ye, but under the circumstances, I can stand in her place if ye'd like."

The truth of their conversation was beginning to dawn on Ceit. "Auntie, I'm no' that naïve. I have my maidenhead." Although, she would have liked to ask her aunt at least ten more questions about the entire process. "May I ask a question?"

"Of course."

"And ye'll no' tell my parents or Grandda?"

Her aunt couldn't contain her smile. "I promise."

Ceit managed to get up the gumption. "Will it really hurt?"

Aunt Brigid lost her smile. "Aye, it does hurt, but when you make love with someone you have strong feelings for, 'tis a wonderful experience. I hope that is how it will be for ye. 'Tis best to choose wisely. Yer time will come."

She shook her head. "I dinnae think so."

Her aunt frowned. "Ye say that with such certainty. Why?"

"Because I dinnae wish to marry. I wish to spend my time working for Scotland. Protecting our land and returning to Ramsay land. I have no interest in living anywhere else."

Her aunt gave her an odd look. "What if I asked ye to stay here on Black Isle."

She shook her head emphatically, but feared speaking as she did not wish to hurt her aunt. Eddirdale Castle was nice, but not as nice as Ramsay Castle.

Aunt Brigid nodded and said, "Dinnae worry. I will no' ask ye." She grinned and a knock sounded at the door.

"Enter," Ceit said.

Dyna stepped inside. "May I have a word with Ceit?"

"Of course," Aunt Brigid said. "Has my husband made any announcement?"

"Aye, he said he willnae be forcing Brin to marry Ceit. Ye didnae know?"

"I did, but I asked him to wait until I spoke with Ceit before announcing it. I wished to know exactly what her wishes were. I'm convinced we have made the right decision."

"Bloody hell, I should hope so," Dyna said. "If ye force something on these two when they are lucky to be alive, we'd have no one willing to patrol. We'd have to have separate forces. One for just women and one for just men. 'Tis most impractical."

Dyna was building into a tirade, though Ceit agreed with her words, but finally her aunt held her hands up in surrender. "Understood, Dyna.

We dinnae wish for that. Ceit will continue on patrol. We willnae ask anything of Brin."

"Good," Dyna barked.

"My thanks, Aunt Brigid," Ceit said.

"If ye have any other questions, Ceit, I'm here for ye."

She nodded and Aunt Brigid closed the door.

Dyna sat down next to her on the bed and said, "Ye are pleased with the results."

"Aye. I am no' interested in marrying Brin or anyone."

Dyna studied her, then said, "Ye wish to continue on patrol? I dinnae wish to take Brigid's word on this."

"Aye, 'tis what I've waited to do forever. I wish to prove myself. Are we continuing?"

"Aye. A report has arrived that there is an English garrison south of the ravine, closer to Grant land. So we will head out on the morrow. Allow the sun to melt more snow as it is strong now. I'd hoped ye'd be willing to come along. Brin will no'. He wishes to stay another sennight with his sisters and Padraig."

"Oh, that makes sense." Why did this overpowering feeling of disappointment course through her insides?

Dyna crossed her arms and her gaze narrowed. "Mayhap ye should have a chat with Brin before ye leave. Alone. Just the two of ye." Dyna patted her knee and stood, taking her leave. "Be at the stable at first light on the morrow. And make sure Jennet or Tara check yer wound before ye leave."

"I promise to do that later. For now, I'll come

with ye," Ceit said. "I need to speak with Brin before I leave."

She hoped she wouldn't regret it, but she had the sudden urge to clear the air with him. Even if all she could see was the look on his face when he turned to tell her to convince her family nothing had transpired between them. He looked as if he hated her, and that expression had nearly stuck a dagger in her belly. So she needed to clear the air between them.

Though she wouldn't tell him the truth.

She was falling in love with him, but she'd never marry him.

CHAPTER SEVENTEEN

BRIN WAS NEAR the stable talking with Maitland when he saw Ceit exit the keep. Her beauty, her stature, always called to him. While he had other desires coursing through him, now was not the time. Instead, they needed to talk. His comment when he'd lost his temper hurt her. That much he observed in her eyes immediately, before she ran out the door of the chamber. It was his fault and he needed to fix it.

He waited to see which direction she was headed until he discovered she was headed straight their way.

"Maitland, excuse me. I believe I need to chat with Ceit. Have ye a suggestion where we could talk privately? I dinnae wish to be accused of anything again."

"Go to the far side of the stable. The lads are all inside so they'll no' bother ye. I willnae go far in case anyone comes along. I agree with yer point of view. If this rumor proves false, we shall return and ye can join our patrol again. Ye were definitely an asset to our group, Brin."

Maitland stepped away and headed to the gates, waving to Ceit as she approached.

Brin strode over to her and asked, "May we talk?"

"Aye," she said. "I came to speak with ye."

He motioned to follow him over to the curtain wall, an isolated area protected from the cold wind from the bay. Once they were alone, he said, "I apologize for any part I had in the trouble between us. And my temper flared with my words. I apologize for that. It was my anger over the situation that drove my temper. We both know we did naught wrong, and to be accused of the worst, of having no honor, upset me more than I care to admit. I hope yer family is no' too upset." Her hands fiddled with her tunic, something he didn't see often. She was still upset, if he were to guess.

"I havenae spoken with Uncle Marcas, but Aunt Brigid is fine. Dyna is more upset about it than I am."

"What we did, what ye experienced, is no' at all what they were asking about. Ye understand the difference?"

"Aye. I have my maidenhead and that is what concerned Uncle Marcas."

His hand reached up and brushed the soft skin of her cheek. "Ye know I would never hurt ye. Aye?"

"I know that, Brin. It was an unfortunate situation—the avalanche, the snowstorm. Even the time of day that it happened. We fought to stay alive. Either way, the two of us alone in the cave should no' cause any undue concern. If so, lasses will never be allowed to go on patrol. It would no' be fair at all."

She licked her lips in the cold, that small movement going right to his traitorous member, something that surprised him. This was not the kind of weather he usually carried erections around in. Blast it all, but it nearly hurt. "I care for ye, Ceit, and I wish circumstances would allow me to pursue a relationship with ye, but I plan to stay. I hear ye have a possible skirmish with an English garrison. Maitland said they are aggressive."

"I heard we are leaving, but Dyna didnae mention that."

"So Maitland said. 'Tis likely to be a wee bit of a battle chasing them back to England. They are too far north."

"But ye are staying here?"

"Aye," he nodded, staring out over the water. "Tara and Riley wished for me to stay, and I told Padraig I'd stay a bit longer. I've no' seen him in a long time."

"I heard he was one of yer closest friends." A breeze whipped inside the curtain wall, hitting them just right. She huddled into her mantle, shivering. "I wish ye a pleasant visit."

He stared at her lips, and when she turned back to face him, he couldn't tear his gaze away. "Even though we arenae betrothed or planning to pursue a relationship, it doesnae mean we canno' enjoy each other's company, does it?"

She locked her gaze on his and took a step closer. "I would like that."

"Ye'll allow me another kiss, my golden beauty?" He noticed a tree nearby, something that would partially hide them from the rest of the people in the courtyard, though there were only one or two about.

"I thought ye'd never ask."

That was all he needed to do what he was desperate to do—have one more taste of the lass. His lips found hers in the winter air, melding against hers and he groaned, a husky sound he wished he'd contained. He wrapped his arms around her and she fell against him, his mouth slanting over hers as he ravaged her mouth with a need so powerful that he didn't recognize it in himself. They belonged together. She tasted of sweet honey and she mimicked every move, his lusty groans finally carrying across the wind.

Maitland's whistle caught him and he let go of her, reluctantly, setting her away from him. "Forgive me, Ceit."

She stepped away with a saucy grin and said, "Naught to forgive. I enjoyed it as much as ye. But since Maitland is coming this way, I'll take my leave."

Ceit hurried away just as Maitland approached.

"Good idea. Get ready to travel at first light, Ceit."

She smiled and ran toward the keep.

Once Maitland was close enough, he said, "Are ye losing yer mind, Cameron? If anyone had seen or heard what I did, ye should be marrying her and bedding her on the morrow. Control yer urges. I thought ye had more sense than that."

Brin shook his head, his gaze following the sway of Ceit's hips all the way to the keep. "I fear she makes me lose all sense, Menzie."

"Then dinnae let her go."

Brin sighed. "It would never work."

"Why no'?"

"Because she said she'd never leave Ramsay land, and I'm heir to the chieftainship in Clan Cameron."

Maitland said, "Ye'll figure it out. Dinnae let her go if ye have those kinds of feelings."

His friend turned and headed back to the keep. "Too cold out here for me."

Brin's hands went to his hips. Was there a way? He only had until the morrow to decide.

~~~

Ceit stepped inside the keep, closing the door and heading straight to the hearth after tossing her mantle on a nearby hook. Kissing Brin was dangerous. She lost track of everything when she was in his arms. Had Maitland not whistled, they'd probably still be locked in that delicious embrace.

What was it about that man that let all her barriers drop? She'd never been so involved with anyone, had never had any interest in sticking her tongue in a man's mouth. Or allowing him to do the same to her.

Jennet came over and whispered, "Locking lips with the right man can cause all kinds of trouble.

If ye have naught else to do, I could use yer help in the healing chamber. And I promise not to mention his name if ye dinnae."

"How…"

"Yer lips are chapped." She pointed to her own lower lip. "Happens in the cold, especially when ye share saliva."

Leave it to her cousin Jennet to describe it so crudely. "I'd be glad to help, but ye'll have to give me some instruction."

Jennet waved her along, so she rubbed her hands together and followed. She loved to walk behind Jennet because she'd done the boldest thing any female had ever done. She'd cut her hair.

It hung to her shoulders, stopping right at her neck. In fact, that was one of the scandalous parts of her bold move because the back of her neck showed at times, especially now that her hair had more curls than ever before and they bounced as she walked, the golden highlights dancing in the sunlight when she was outdoors.

Once they entered the chamber, Tara said, "Ye brought help, I hope, Ceit? We surely could use it. Brigid has another one in labor, so Riley went with her. We have all these men who need their bandages changed, and Giselle is worried about the bairn. Thinks she's not eating enough. I can work with her if ye two can handle the bandages."

Ceit said, "I'd be glad to help wherever I can."

Jennet nodded and said to Tara, "We'll handle it. Go help Giselle. We need that wee lassie growing. She had a risky beginning."

Tara disappeared so Jennet pointed to a stool

for her to take at the table. "There are three men waiting outside to come in. If ye help me with the first one, ye may be able to do the next one by yerself. I'll be here for questions."

"I like that idea, but what about Lynie? Is she struggling?"

"Giselle isn't sure she's feeding enough. She thinks Lynie is sleeping too much. That can be for several reasons. Poor Giselle had such a traumatic birth, and the bairn a traumatic start in life. Mayhap the baby is falling asleep at the nipple and isn't feeding long enough. Or they might need a little help learning how to get Lynie to latch on properly so she gets enough milk. And we've had some babes prefer goat's milk through a false nipple we create. It doesnae matter where the milk comes from as long as they continue to eat. Newborns are hard work but they are so worth it. And Tara is good with the new mothers. She'll help them figure it out."

The door opened and a man came in Ceit didn't recognize. "Over here, Duncan. We'll change yer bandage right here at the table."

Jennet was verra organized, showing Ceit all their supplies. "Ethan likes to help me. Ye'll find in this container various sizes of linen strips. He's imagined every size possible, just changes each set by a wee bit and cuts more. Considers it his duty and I love it! I dinnae think I'll ever have to cut another set." She explained the different ointments and poultices, each in a different container. Then they set to replacing Duncan's bandage.

They removed one and the poor man winced, but Jennet said, "We'll no' take long, Duncan."

Ceit peered closely at it, then pointed to the middle. "Is that no' some pus still there?"

Jennet looked closer. "Good catch. I believe ye are correct. More ointment, Duncan. And some potion to keep the fever away. Come back in two days."

They worked for several hours after a new injury came in, and Ceit was surprised to find that dusk was nearly upon them. Jennet left and said, "I'll be right back."

"When ye return, would ye mind checking my wound, Jennet?"

"Aye. I'll take a look and change the bandage if ye like." Then she disappeared.

Ceit looked around the chamber, surprised at how much she had enjoyed working with Jennet. She was efficient and a good teacher. The men had been grateful for all they did. Perhaps healing wouldn't be such a bad purpose in life. Did she have the gift for it? She didn't know yet.

Jennet returned quickly with two trenchers and said, "Ye have to eat. Ye'll be on patrol with that lousy dried meat and oatcakes. I'll clean the table and we can eat there, unless ye'd like to eat in the hall."

They were the only two people left in the chamber so Ceit said, "Nay, I'd prefer here. Everyone will be staring at me if I eat out there."

Jennet cleaned an area for them, then settled. "I have an idea how ye are feeling, but may I give ye some advice, Ceit?"

"Sure. I would love some. I havenae had the chance to speak with Isla."

"She's pretty hard to pull away from Grif."

Ceit took a bite of her food then waited for Jennet to say something, her curiosity piqued. She didn't chat with her cousin alone much. Jennet finally stopped fussing with the food and said, "Dinnae let him get away."

Ceit tipped her head, surprised at Jennet's words.

"Ye seem to suit each other well. And I was outside and happened to catch that short kiss. Ye are attracted to each other, Brin is a good man, he eventually will be chieftain. Ye surely arenae far from Ramsay land, much closer than we are. If ye have any inkling that ye are going to fall in love with him, then dinnae let him get away."

She didn't know what to say, so said the most honest thing she could think of, "I'm just confused."

Jennet nodded and said, "I'm no' surprised. Think on my words. Ye'll see him again, I'm sure. Shall we speak of something else? Are ye interested in healing at all, Ceit? Ye did a fine job as my assistant."

"I liked it more than I expected I would." That was another honest statement.

"Ye should work with Aunt Brenna whenever ye get the opportunity. She's the best. Ye have a natural curiosity that most dinnae have."

"What do ye mean?"

"Ye can look at the most disgusting wound, and it doesnae bother ye. 'Tis rare."

"Truly?"

"Aye. Most people would heave after looking at some of the wounds ye did. Ye acted like it was a usual occurrence." Then Jennet leaned forward and whispered, "Dinnae let him go."

Honesty was rearing its head again. She whispered back, "I dinnae want to."

That was the most honest statement she'd made in a long time.

CHAPTER EIGHTEEN

THE PATROL LEFT at first light the next day.
Ceit had secretly hoped that Brin would
change his mind about joining them, but he
wasn't outside when the group gathered. She'd
done as Dyna had said, getting her wound taken
care of by Jennet. Her leg had healed nicely, but
Jennet had put some salve on it just to be safe.
She'd also given Ceit a small amount to carry
along with her on the patrol.

They were down to eight in their group. Thea,
Wenna, Ceit, and Dyna would be the archers.
Tevis, Alaric, Maitland, and Willum would be
swordsmen. How she prayed their numbers would
be enough. Dobbin was the messenger traveling
between the clans to keep them updated on the
English movement.

Isla and Grif had stayed back with Brin as
they'd said they would do. The couple intended
to join the patrol again in the future, but not until
they'd had a visit at Eddirdale Castle. Ysenda and
Lewis were stuck healing, with the promise that
the patrol would return for them in a moon or

two. Broken bones took their time healing. They were all aware of that.

Ceit knew Uncle Gavin and Aunt Merewen wouldn't be happy that Ysenda was forced to stay behind, but he'd receive word and if Ceit were to guess, he would probably travel to visit soon. Mayhap they'd be on Black Isle for the Yuletide.

The patrol headed out as the sun came up in a cloudless sky, something they hoped would remain for the day since it promised to melt more snow. Thea rode next to her with Wenna behind them. She hadn't befriended Wenna yet, but she needed to get to know her better. She just hadn't had the chance.

Thea said, "That avalanche had to have been frightening for ye and Brin. From where I was, I saw Ysenda and Lewis get hit and the two flew down the mountain, bouncing in such a way that I feared they'd not survive. Could ye see that?"

"Nay. We saw the avalanche, the snow and rocks barreling down the side of the ravine, but I never saw anyone fall. My horse nearly went down with the rocks, but Brin's fast actions kept it from going over, though she turned skittish. I had to ride Brin's horse back to the cave with him because my mount was so unsettled by the avalanche. Maitland used the bird call to let us know everyone was hale, though he must not have known about Ysenda yet. How long were ye there?" She couldn't imagine how awful it would be to go over the side of the ravine. And then to break a bone and find yourself at the bottom of the ravine? Inconceivable.

"Surprisingly enough, none of the horses went over the edge," Thea explained. "That fact probably saved them both from being crushed. Maitland split the group, sent Dyna on ahead to get a cart to get them back if necessary. He and Willum climbed into the gorge and brought them both up. Lewis was badly bruised so he was able to limp with help. They didnae discover his break until later. Ysenda had to be carried. She tried so hard to hold in her tears, but after a while, they came out."

Wenna called out from behind them, "I cried for her when I saw her misshapen leg. I know Jennet and Tara had to spend some time trying to straighten the bone, something that was truly painful for Ysenda. I hope she'll heal straight."

Ceit said, "I dread traveling back through the ravine. Poor Ysenda and Lewis."

To their surprise, the ravine was clear except for a few more rocks on the path. The snow had melted and they cleared the area with no problem. The group made a stop midday to refresh the horses and to have a bite to eat. Unexpectedly, there was no snow once they were an hour south of the ravine.

Snow—unpredictable, beautiful, deadly.

The sky was clear as they moved about in the small clearing, Maitland and Dyna discussing the information they'd received and deciding how to approach.

Ceit and Thea stood close enough to listen in.

"Dyna, we're split evenly between archers and swordsmen. We have to arrange them as we ride or we'll be in trouble. Ye canno' have the archers riding together in the front. Ye must split them so if we are attacked from the forest, the swordsmen can make sure the archers have a chance to set themselves."

"Do ye believe what we've heard? Do ye think the English are attacking from the forest? I thought they were after castles, that they would be trying to overtake one specific castle. Control it for England."

Maitland paced, his hands on his hips. "I dinnae know what to believe. Dobbin's message was that they were a group of English reivers, not a garrison. And they numbered less than a score. They arenae dressed as soldiers, but instead are hiding in the trees. 'Tis only when they speak that the Scots learn they are English. But how did they get this far north?"

Dyna said, "'Tis the only way they've made it this far. They would have to hide in the trees or a couple of clans would work together to overtake them and send them home. The Grant contingency alone could take on a small garrison in a couple of hours. 'Tis the only possible way they could have made it this far. Deceit, treachery, and cunning. We must be more deceitful and more cunning. As simple as that."

He stopped his pacing to face her. "Fine, I'll agree. Ye set up the order of the riders. They must be able to react quickly. We'll leave in a quarter hour. I must find the bushes." Maitland left and Dyna went in the opposite direction.

Ceit couldn't help but feel a wee bit of excitement about this situation. They'd be patrolling like they usually did. She hoped the enemy number wasn't too large or they'd struggle to overtake them. But not a large garrison was a blessing in her mind. This was her chance to prove her skills.

Thea muttered, "If I dinnae know better, I'd think ye were pleased."

"I am," Ceit said. "Are ye no' pleased that we are facing less than a score instead of a group of three score?"

Thea said, "Nay. If it were three score, we'd no' engage. Less than a score and we will engage."

Wenna asked, "But I thought we were just to watch the English, not engage them."

Ceit said, "True for the Lowlands. But no one wants the bastards in the Highlands, especially this far north, so 'tis our duty to send them back."

"In case they are part of a larger group that has arranged to meet at a spot north of us. We canno' allow them to have large numbers here." Thea rubbed her arms as she shivered in the cold. "Especially in the winter months. No one will suspect them."

Maitland returned and motioned for the group to mount up. "Dobbin said this group is less than two hours south of us. Be aware. They are hiding in the woods, looking to overtake anyone. They seem to be a rogue group of English fighting for weapons and coin. Dyna will arrange us so stay in the order she assigns. The swordmen will attack while the lasses set up their bows. We need both to take them on. Be aware of yer surroundings and dinnae move about."

The patrol headed south, their casual conversation ended until they located the English. They needed to be alert and aware. Ceit had to admit that knowing they were close to a skirmish with the English caused her palms to sweat even in the cold. Her eyes darted back and forth and all she could think of was her grandmother questioning her sight.

She could see just fine, dammit. Hell, how she'd wished her grandmother hadn't planted those doubts in her mind. The only way to prove the woman wrong was to show her strength on the battlefield. She would prove herself to be as mighty an archer as the famous Gwyneth Ramsay.

She'd show them all, including Brin. She wished he'd come along.

Dammit all to hell, but she missed him.

They continued in silence, listening to the sounds of the forest. They had to be ready to battle. Would they know before they were attacked? They surely would sense it, would they not? This sense of anticipation, of impending doom, would not leave her. Someday she'd asked those older and wiser how they handled waiting patiently for battle. Waiting for the imminent attack.

For the one moment an arrow could sluice through the air and land in the middle of your chest before you were aware of any marauders.

She wished to scream her displeasure with this game of chase, of creating the element of surprise, of catching the enemy hiding…somewhere.

This game of life and death. Of the English against the Scots. Of only the strong will survive. Was she one of the strong?

Ceit had a sudden sinking feeling deep in her belly. Deep. Deeper than she'd ever experienced before. A pair of blue eyes popped into her mind. She should never have left Brin, wished he were next to her right this moment. The man had stolen her heart, and she had let him walk away.

All because she wished to be the best archer in the world, have the same reputation her dear grandmother had, and believed she had to remain on Ramsay land to accomplish such a thing. Why did she think living on Cameron land would prevent her from practicing her archery?

She was about to go into battle and every problem she'd had in the last moon popped into her mind. At this point, she could barely think straight much less see straight. Fool. Sometimes she was just a fool.

Unlike her grandmother who had guessed Ceit's greatest fear was coming to fruition— losing her eagle-like sight. She didn't understand the whole process of a person's eyes worsening as they grew older, but her grandmother had the same problem. Was that to be her destiny, to follow in her grandmother's footsteps when it came to her vision?

Her grandmother suggested her sight was going, but she didn't wish to believe it or accept that it could be true. How could she become a great archer if she couldn't see her target?

Dyna held her hand up to slow their progress,

tipping her head toward the forest to their right. She was correct. The rustle of horses and riders was as clear as the sun in the sky at the moment.

Dyna waved them back, motioning for the archers to get into position. Ceit searched for a good tree to climb, but there weren't many, the landscape full of bushes instead of trees. Thea was already in one, and Wenna had begun to climb into the only other one. There were no other trees around.

Sweat broke out on her brow as a group of Englishmen broke through the trees, swords aimed straight at them.

And bows. She couldn't guess how many yet, but they were definitely outnumbered. Since when did the English have mounted bowmen? Their archers usually marched so they could remain stable. It took special skill to shoot mounted.

As Ramsay guards, Ceit and the others had received countless hours of training, first in the field, then endless practice on horseback with Grandsire hollering at you if you missed.

The first arrow sluiced in the air so close to her head that she cursed as loud as she could, "Dammit, ye ugly bastard! Ye think ye can take me down? Ye are wrong." Visions of the people she loved, all the ones who'd trained her for so many years danced across her mind—their teachings bringing her to this point. Her father telling her to have confidence. Her mother telling her to not fear men, but to challenge them instead. Her grandfather telling her she had the skill and the might in her blood.

Her blood! The blood that was not meant to be spilled on this Highland ground.

And Brin. The kindest, gentlest man in the entire world telling her she was beautiful and holding her as if she were the most precious thing in the land.

Chaos reigned as Dyna pulled her horse behind the two trees so she could fire, firing arrows faster than anyone. Maitland charged with his sword along with Alaric and Tevis, while Willum went to the right, taking men down in quick succession. She followed them, easily able to shoot at the fool who was coming straight for her.

Straight toward her. If she didn't kill him now, she'd be dead.

She slowed and aimed directly at him, then let the arrow fly.

CHAPTER NINETEEN

B RIN SAT IN the great hall of Eddirdale Castle, chatting with both sisters and Padraig. All of a sudden, he bolted out of his seat. His sister's head rolled back and he caught her just in time, kept her from falling from her bench. Whenever Riley had one of her dreams of sight where she saw something that was about to happen, she did the same thing. It frightened all of them no matter how often it happened.

"Riley!" Tara shouted.

Riley's head fell to the side while Brin held her seated on the bench. It was a few moments before she regained consciousness, the poor thing lifting her head in confusion before her gaze locked on Brin.

Brin's eyes misted. "I know what caused it."

"What is it, Brin?" Tara asked.

"I know what ye must do. The question is do ye, Brin?" Riley leaned back and crossed her arms. "Are ye going to accept it yet?"

"What are ye talking about?" Tara asked. "If ye are seeing something, ye must tell yer sister, especially if 'tis about our brother." Her pursed lips told Brin she wouldn't budge on this demand.

"What is happening?" Padraig asked.

"Riley just had a moment, saw something in a dream, and it has to do with Brin. What is it? Ye two must tell us what ye know."

Brin took a seat next to Riley, keeping his arm around her to make sure she didn't fall back again. "I saw her too."

Riley looked to her sister and explained, "Ceit needs him. She's in trouble. And…"

"Ye can see that?" Padraig asked. "And ye saw it too, Brin?"

"Aye, I didnae see her, but I have this overpowering need to leave. See that she is hale."

"If Riley saw it, ye can believe it, Brin. Ye must go to her." Tara grabbed Riley's hand and squeezed it, straightening the hairs on her head that had fallen askew.

"What the hell? Is it because ye were so close to her that ye had the same dream, Brin?" Padraig asked.

"I dinnae know for sure, but I canno' ignore it." Brin got up to leave but stopped. "Ye know I must go to her. Riley, ye said something else but never finished. And what?"

Riley took a deep breath before turning around to look at her brother. "She loves ye, Brin. I can feel it in her heart. She's yer soulmate." Riley sobbed the last sentence out, then let her head drop to the table. "Go and dinnae wait. Ye could be too late."

Brin prayed she was wrong.

CHAPTER TWENTY

CEIT HAD TO fire before the English swordsmen were close enough to strike her. Everything slowed, her horse now moving in what Uncle Alex used to say was fighting mode. She guided him with her knees so she could send off a slew of arrows at the enemy—especially the two on horseback headed straight for her, their swords reflecting in the sunlight. She fired and fired, hitting one rider direct in the belly, knocking him off his horse. The other rider hollered and fired at her, catching her in the shoulder.

The pain ripped through her and she hissed to keep from screaming. She left the arrow in her shoulder lest she bleed to death from pulling it out. Gritting her teeth to hang on, she reached for the reins again to keep her horse stable. She couldn't stop or she'd be dead. The man yelled with delight at his hit.

Ceit's gaze scanned the entire area, counting the number against them, clearly seeing they were still outnumbered. They'd taken down some of the English but her team was still all upright and fighting. She thought of the slice she'd taken in her leg, praying the same would not happen this time. The arrow in her shoulder wouldn't do the damage the sword had.

Would it?

The activity around her changed even more—everything now appearing in slow motion. Everything except her mind that was jumping from one thought to the next faster than a bolt of lightning shooting from the sky.

Brin.

The English bastard's widening smile, the man who'd hit her.

Men everywhere battling.

And she got angry. This was the second time she'd been hit, and she didn't like it. She didn't deserve it! Dammit all to hell and back, but she was stronger and better than the enemy.

She gritted her teeth and nocked another arrow with a bellow of rage, the pain from the arrow lodged in her flesh like a hot dagger sinking deeper and deeper. With her head tipped back, she cursed at every indignity in her world. Getting wounded in her leg, her shoulder, nearly freezing to death in a cave, accused of being inappropriate, the possibility of losing her sight. And the wicked arrow ripping her shoulder to shreds as she moved. Dammit!

Ignore it. Ignore it. She was stronger than this.

What would Grandmama do?

Kill the bastard!

She pulled back on the bow and aimed, hissing at the pain. She missed her target but hit another rider on his flank, knocking him off the horse. Reaching back for another arrow with a scream, she nocked again, her horse now responding to her emotions but holding hard, his blows threatening to anyone coming near her.

The bastard who hit her was nearly on her, so she howled through the pain. "Ye canno' stop me!" Her horse sensed her pain and lifted onto his hind legs as if to send a warning to anyone coming at them. They landed with a curse and she bellowed again. "Ye arenae even as brave as my grandmother!" The words felt better than the scream. "Come on, come on, ye surly bastard." She let the arrow fly and hit the man behind her target.

The blood trickled down her arm in a meandering river now visible as she moved, but she had to ignore it. She shook off the bit of blood on her hand with a curse and a bellow. "Get off me!"

Grabbing her bow again with her wounded arm, she nocked, aimed, and hit the bastard in the leg, his horse feeling the vibration and rearing on its hind legs, sending him off its back and onto the ground, hard.

She cheered and her horse reared in response, and she barely managed to hang on, again shrieking from the pain in her shoulder as she grabbed the reins. "Ach, who else wants to fight me?"

The English's numbers had dwindled.

"I dare ye! Come at me, fool!"

One man took one look at her and turned tail,

heading back into the forest. Two more came for her, joined by a third from the other side. She brushed the sweat from her brow with her good hand and grabbed another arrow, sending her horse into a full gallop.

Her vision dimmed, but she shook her head. *Nay, my vision is fine, Grandmama! Stop saying it isn't.*

The three men looked like five men from the sweat dripping into her eyes. She nocked her arrow and shot into the middle of them, a shout of pain telling her she'd hit one. Where the hell were they coming from? Or were they leaving?

Then they suddenly disappeared.

A voice called to her from behind her. "Stop yer horse, MacAdam."

Another familiar voice, "Ceit, stop. Ye are hurt!"

Maitland came along behind her and lifted her off her horse, onto his lap. "Ceit, ye have to stop. Ye scared them more than my sword did. Yer horse is foaming. Enough. They've all turned tail and run from ye. Though we killed more than half of them."

She glanced at her horse, seeing Dyna take the reins of her dear horse and guiding him off to the side.

Maitland turned his horse around and slowed, joining another one and handing her over. "Brin, ye must be a seer. She's all yers. Get her back to the clearing, and we'll treat her there."

Brin shook his head. "Just for a quick assessment. Then I'm taking her straight to Grant land. She's lost too much blood. Her tunic is drenched. Follow me so we can tie above it, slow the bleeding."

"Go ahead to the clearing. I'll be right behind ye. There's water there, and we can try to get the arrow out and bind her to slow the blood loss."

"No more than a quarter hour, then we have to go. I'll get her to drink. Mama says it's a must."

"Brin?" She glanced up, thinking she saw an angel. One who was much better looking than the English.

"Aye, my love. I have ye." He tugged her close and said, "Hang on. We cannae go slow."

And just like that, all was wonderful again. She hugged him and sobbed into his broad chest. "I'll take care of ye, lass. I'll no' leave ye again."

"He hit me. My shoulder. How bad is it? It hurts really bad. Am I going to lose my arm?"

"Nay, ye've lost blood, so ye must drink while we get the arrow out, then we're going straight to Grant Castle. Only about an hour's ride from here." She could feel the warmth of his hand even through the fabric of her clothing. Or was she imagining it? Was she imagining Brin? Or dreaming?

She was definitely going daft. "I'd like to go find that bastard who hit me." She sniffled, trying to slow the tears.

"Lass, I think ye paid him back. I saw a man fly off his horse once he was hit."

"Good. He…deserved…it." She sobbed in between her words, her breath hitching.

"Where is the clearing?" he asked.

"I dinnae know. I cannae see because of sweat dripping in my eyes."

Maitland came abreast of him, Dyna behind him. "To yer right up ahead. Past that big oak."

Once they stopped, Brin lifted her down to Maitland who carried her over to a large rock before handing her back to Brin after he sat down.

Brin said, "Dyna, grab the skin of water, please. Maitland and I will get the arrow out. 'Tis verra high in her shoulder. I should be able to tie above in her armpit to slow the blood flow."

Maitland said, "I'm so glad ye are a Cameron and know exactly what to do. But ye know as well as I do that we have to get the head of the arrow out."

Ceit stared up at Maitland's serious expression just before he touched the arrow, causing her to yelp. "Nay, 'twill hurt too much. Will it no' just slip out?"

Dyna and Maitland both grimaced, but neither said anything.

"Hell, 'tis no' easy. Mayhap I can reach in and get it out." Ceit's hand found the part of the arrow embedded in her flesh. She ran her fingers around the edge until the realization came to her that she couldn't do it. In fact, she didn't want anyone touching her because the pain was nearly unbearable. She tried again, but after three failed attempts, she collapsed against Brin, the tears starting again. But she would not give in.

Ceit sat up stronger, wanting to make sure she had some control over the situation, maintain the ability to push whoever dared to touch her away. But it was too difficult. She was weakening and she didn't like it. Even her mind was doing things she didn't like, her sudden inability to focus and speak coherently was more than she could handle. She leaned her head onto Brin's shoulder, giving up, but silently loving that she could take in his scent. It calmed her more than she would ever admit to anyone. Brin would take care of her, of that much she was certain.

Dyna said, "I wish we could knock her out."

"Go ahead. I can handle it," Ceit mumbled.

"Knocking ye out or removing the arrow?" Brin asked with a chuckle, placing a chaste kiss on her forehead.

"The arrow," she muttered. "Just yank it out. I trust ye."

Dyna said, "I dinnae know. She's lost quite a bit of blood. This may prove to be too much for her."

"Mayhap nay then," she said, jerking her head back up, wondering if Dyna was right. "Leave it be."

"Lass," Maitland said as he patted her head fondly, pushing it back to Brin's shoulder. "I might think it was too much for ye, but since we all just watched ye shoot up five Englishmen with an arrow in yer shoulder, I think ye can handle it."

"I did? That many?" She had a vague recollection of battle, but all she seemed to recall was how much her arm hurt. Or was it her shoulder?

Dyna said, "Ceit MacAdam, ye were firing with such accuracy that ye sent half of their cavalry in the opposite direction. The only one who truly dared to take ye on was the one next to the first one ye killed. He had vengeance all over his face when he charged ye, but ye managed to knock him off his mount twice."

"I killed someone?" She closed her eyes, unwilling to think on that at the moment.

Brin said, "No one knows for sure." He kissed her forehead and said, "We can talk about this all later, but Maitland and I are going to pull that arrow out. 'Tis going to hurt quite a bit, but we have to get it out. We canno' travel with it in yer arm, or it could do worse damage."

"I'm ready. Get it out." She felt the tie just below her armpit, then closed her eyes and held her breath as they poked and probed a bit.

Maitland said, "Dyna, yer fingers are smaller. I can see the one side of the tip. If ye can grab it, ye can get it out in less than a minute. She can handle the pain for a few moments."

The others arrived and gathered around them.

Thea said, "Ceit, ye were a wild archer out there. I've never seen ye like that. They were all afraid of ye."

Brin held his hand up and Thea stopped talking, moving closer to see exactly what they were doing.

Dyna peered at the point of impact and said, "Bloody hell, I canno' see it. Point it out again, Maitland? Which side do ye see it on?"

Thea said, "I can do it. I've taken many out of animals. My mother taught me how."

They all turned to face her and Ceit said, "Thea,

please." She knew Thea worked beautifully with any animal, both calmly and efficiently.

Thea bent down and peered at the wound. "Dyna, pour the water over my hands, please."

Dyna did as she asked. Then Thea whispered to her, "I'll touch and move it quickly. That part will hurt, Ceit, but after all ye just did, I think ye can handle it. Just keep yer tongue inside yer mouth and not between yer teeth. Scream if ye like."

Ceit nodded, doing as she said. Thea reached in and found the tip right away, or so she guessed since the pain became nearly unbearable. "'Tis it," she hollered. "Ye've found it."

"And I've got it." Thea held it up for all to see, then Brin poured more water on her wound and held a clean linen square on it, pushing hard to stop the bleeding.

Ceit passed out.

CHAPTER TWENTY-ONE

BRIN STOOD IN the Grant healing chamber, unable to tear his gaze from the slight form in the bed, settled and tucked in. Connor, Jamie, and Gracie were with him.

Gracie said, "I think she'll be fine, Brin. But as ye know, we'll no' know until she awakens. Blood loss is still a mysterious thing to healers. When have they lost too much? I dinnae know."

"Neither does Mama." He paced across the chamber but found his steps were not as strong and straight as they should be. "I think I could use some sleep. Will she sleep for a bit?"

"Aye, I gave her a wee bit of sleeping potion, something that will help with her pain also. Ye may sleep in here if ye wish."

Thinking on all that transpired before, he said, "Probably better if I sleep in the stables."

"Stables?" Connor snorted. "We have a chamber for ye on the second floor. Our guest chamber. 'Tis all made up. The others who were on patrol with ye. Are they coming along behind ye?"

"Nay, they are going after the ones we

missed. Mayhap I'd take an ale before I find my bedchamber. Do ye mind, Connor?"

Gracie fussed around the chamber and said, "Connor will find ye a meat pie. There were some left from the evening meal. Should hold ye until the morrow."

"Many thanks to ye, Gracie."

Jamie asked with a smirk, "So she fights like her mother and grandmother?"

"Aye. Maitland said she scared half the group away. The ones left after she hit several with her arrows. The arrow in her shoulder never stopped her."

Jamie clasped his shoulder as he guided him toward the door. "I see an interest more than just a passing one. Am I correct, Brin?"

"Aye. She's much younger than me, but I dinnae seem to care."

Gracie said, "Age doesnae matter. Now we just have to find one for Maeve. Ye are pursuing Ceit, truly?"

Brin nodded. "I'm drawn to the lass. I wished to fight it, but no more."

Jamie chuckled as he held the door for him. "Sounds like true love to me! Ye grab yer ale, and I'll help Gracie clean up here. Stay as long as ye like."

Brin followed Connor into the great hall, taking the proffered goblet before he settled in front of the hearth, the dying embers just enough to warm him.

"Ye'd make a fine match with Ceit, I think. Does she feel the same?"

"Aye and nay. We suit each other, but she doesnae wish to leave Ramsay land, and I am destined to be chieftain, though Cameron land is much quieter than Grant land. Ye are kept busy here because yer clan is so large. Judge the sheer number of guards ye train every day is larger than my whole clan. All is quiet near us. I fear I may be bored taking over for my sire."

"I know better than anyone that there is more to running a clan than ye think," Connor explained, banking the fire before he sat down again. "Have yerself a few bairns, and ye'll no longer be bored."

"Truly?"

A serving lass brought out two meat pies, one for each, so she set the platter down on the small table between them and took her leave. "Many thanks, lass. Go home," Connor called out after her.

"Many thanks to ye, Chief." The door closed behind her.

Connor took a bit of his meat pie, chewed a bit, then asked, "Anyone else injured? My daughter hale?"

"Aye, the rest are hale, but anxious to finish what they started with that group of English reivers."

"Good. Tell me. What do ye wish for in yer life, Brin? Have ye never loved a lass?"

"I did once," he admitted, chewing on his meat pie. "But she rejected me for another. I thought I always wished to be a chieftain, like ye and Jamie, Torrian, the kind others look up to. But

Cameron land? 'Tis no' much happening on Cameron land."

"So guarding our Lord's abbey isnae enough for ye? There have been many years when the abbey has been attacked. All it takes is one fool to talk about the treasure, then everyone wants it. Ask Maitland's sire. He'll tell ye about the time they all wanted to go after the treasure. Since then it has quieted. I think it was yer sire's treasure for yer mother that ended it all."

"My sire's treasure?"

"Aye, he ordered something from Europe for yer mother. Ye must have heard the tale many times. Word got around that it was a treasure of gems or something similar. Everyone wished to grab it before it was delivered. Imagine their dismay when paper was delivered instead of a gemstone." He chuckled. "Wish I could have seen that. My sire spoke of how disappointed everyone was in the keep when Uncle Aedan presented the gifts to Aunt Jennie."

"Of course I recall that. The monks travel so much that 'twas easy to do. So may I be bold enough to ask ye what ye think yer purpose is in this life? I've been thinking on that and I admit I'm confused."

Connor leaned back in his chair, his large frame filling the piece of furniture built specifically for his sire. "My purpose. I suppose I could come up with a few for ye. I used to think 'twas to help Mama take care of Papa, but he outlived her by many years. Then I think 'twas to marry Sela, save her from her life of hell. She often tells me so."

"'Tis true. Amazing that ye were interested in her from the verra beginning." He'd heard the tale of the master spider villain.

"Aye, but then I tell her that our purpose together was to produce Dyna, along with our other bairns. But Dyna has such an impact on so many. And with her seeing abilities, she took over much of my time when she was younger. Now my purpose is two-fold."

"Aye?"

"Aye. As chieftain of Clan Grant, and then my favorite of all."

He tipped his head, unable to think what that would be.

"That of Grandpapa. I love it. Wee Thora and Sylvi and Sandor. They keep my life busy. And Sela loves being Grandmama."

"Hard to say which is the most important, is it no'?"

"I dinnae know. But I tell ye so ye recognize that being chieftain of yer clan is only part of yer purpose in this world. I think ye have a lass who needs ye to find her. Ye will have bairns who need ye for one reason or another, and yer parents will need ye as they age. 'Twas an honor to take care of my sire after he had difficulty walking. Dinnae discount that in yer value." Connor set his chair back down and stared at the flames. "I still have much left to do, though I know no' exactly what it is. Ye should ask yer sister. As a seer, does she no' tell ye anything?"

"Aye, she did."

Connor cocked a brow at him. "And…"

"Riley says Ceit is my soulmate."

Connor chuckled, then leaned forward to clasp Brin's shoulder. "'Tis the best guidance ye could ever ask for. Guidance from a seer who is related to ye. Take it from the sire of a seer. They know of what they speak."

He couldn't argue with Connor. "Yer words ring true. I think I must have a chat with Ceit when she awakens."

"I agree. And dinnae busy yerself running around the pine trees. Go straight for the one in the middle. The tallest one. Ceit MacAdam."

CHAPTER TWENTY-TWO

CEIT OPENED HER eyes, memories flooding her mind as to all that had happened. She stared up at the ceiling in the chamber she was in, an unrecognizable one, trying to recall where she was.

What the hell had happened?

She moved her upper body and winced at the shooting pain in her left shoulder. Or her arm. Or somewhere. Then she wiggled her legs as a test, and sure enough, the pain in her leg from the sword slice in battle was still there.

Perhaps it was worse. She swallowed, hoping to moisten her dry throat so she could speak, but it was too dry. Her gaze looked about for the source of the voices, finally locking on one she recognized. "Brin?"

Brin came into her view, looking as handsome as ever.

"Where am I?" She grabbed his hand and gripped him tightly.

Her father appeared on her other side. "Ceit? How do ye feel?"

"Terrible," she croaked. "Water, please?"

Gracie Grant pushed her sire back gently and stepped in front of him with a goblet of water. "Brin, help her to sit a wee bit. Ceit, 'tis a wonderful thing that ye are thirsty. Drink as much as ye like." Then she spoke to a lass near the door. "Some warm bone broth, please."

Brin placed his arm underneath her back and propped her up while someone else came along and placed a pillow under her back. She took two sips of the cool beverage then fell back onto the pillow. "What happened? Where am I?"

Brin mopped her brow and said, "Ye were in battle against a group of Englishmen acting more like border reivers. Ye took an arrow to yer shoulder and Thea removed the tip, but ye lost too much blood so I brought ye here to Grant land. Ye needed stitching in both yer arm and yer leg. Ye opened up the wound in yer leg again, so 'tis why ye hurt so. Gracie can give ye something to ease the pain."

"Nay, no' yet. Papa, why are ye here?" She wasn't surprised to be on Grant land, but why would her sire be here? And was that her brother behind him?

"Yer mother made me come. Maitland and Dyna stopped to tell us of yer injury so she gave me no choice in the matter. Cadyn insisted on coming along too."

"And the others? They are hale?"

Cadyn came forward and leaned over to speak with her. "They are all hale. Chasing the reiver group south when they stopped. Said ye were wild at the skirmish. Nice job, Ceit."

She frowned, her mind returning to the battle. How she hadn't had a tree to climb so had fought straight on. Killed a man and the man next to him had fired an arrow and hit her on the shoulder. And there were men everywhere, but she had kept nocking her arrows, a fury inside her fueling an anger she'd never had. What had caused it? Was it just her temper reacting to her injuries? She couldn't recall for sure.

Her father said, "Maitland said he had to stop ye after ye scared off the remaining group of marauders. Said ye were possessed with a drive to finish the battle unlike any he'd ever seen."

The pain in her leg increased. She looked from her father to her brother and back to Brin. "Why are ye here? Ye chose to stay on Black Isle."

"Because I had a feeling, and my sister had a dream that ye needed me. So I followed and just in time. Do ye no' recall me in the clearing with Maitland and Dyna?"

She did, bits and pieces, portions of screams in the battle returning to her. The massive amount of blood on the field. "Many thanks for coming to my rescue, Brin." She did the best she could to smile, but even that small effort proved difficult. She didn't know what else to say to him with her sire and brother right there listening.

Brin sat on the stool next to the bed. "Ceit, the last thing I did was rescue ye. Ye are a fierce warrior on yer own. Ye didnae need my help in battle, but I am glad I was there to help with yer injuries and see ye to Grant land safely.

Her sire said, "Many thanks for bringing her here, Cameron."

"Where's Mama?" She had this intense need for her mother, something she didn't wish to try to explain to anyone.

"She's home with Tryana and Lainey." Her father brushed her hair back and kissed her forehead.

"I want to go home. Take me home, Papa. Brin, ye are welcome to come along if ye like." She couldn't beg him to travel with her as long as her sire was still there.

Gracie had stepped back, but her face appeared again. "I'm afraid no' quite yet, lass. Ye need to heal a wee bit more. We have to get ye walking again or ye'll never make it back."

Brin said, "Ceit, ye took a major step back losing the blood ye did. Ye will have to gain yer strength back to travel. But as soon as ye are ready, I'll escort ye back."

"I'll be waiting," her father said. "Brin can travel with us, if he likes, but I'm no' leaving until ye are ready to travel. Gracie must give her approval before we'll take our leave. I'm proud of ye, Ceit. They say ye fought hard and true. Said Grandpapa and Grandmama would be verra proud of ye. Dyna said she'd tell all to them."

She nodded, then a compelling need to close her eyes overwhelmed her. She whispered, "I'm tired."

Gracie asked, "Can ye sleep or do ye need some of my sleeping potion to help yer pain?"

Would she appear weak if she asked for

something to ease the pain? Brin leaned over and whispered, "Take it. 'Tis a fine healing potion too. Mama believes 'twill help ye heal faster. Sleep is good."

"I'll take some. Just a wee bit." She hated to seem so weak, but she also could scream with pain if she were alone. And the more she awakened, the more it hurt, enough that she could roll back and forth and tug every hair from her head.

"And the next time ye awaken, we'll get ye some porridge for yer belly," Gracie said, helping her to drink some warm broth.

The last thing on her mind was food.

All she wanted to do was go home.

Brin squeezed her hand and said to her sire, "I'll stay with her. Go get some food. Ye just arrived."

Cadyn said, "I'm going, Papa. I'm starving."

Cadyn's father said, "I'll meet ye there in a few moments. Go ahead and get yer fill while ye can, but leave something for me." Once Cadyn was gone, his father said, "Hell, but 'tis nearly impossible to fill that lad's belly."

Brin laughed. "He's got a solid muscular build to feed. Ye can tell he works with his sword often." Cadyn wasn't the tallest he'd met, especially on Grant land where the men grew like trees, but he did have one of the broadest set of shoulders he'd ever seen.

Cailean said, "The boy lifts boulders for fun. I'm pleased he found Tryana to distract him to do other things besides eating and lifting."

Brin had to laugh at the image he had of Ceit's brother lifting boulders over his head. But his grin left him when Cailean said what was on his mind. "I see an interest in ye more than that of one of the members in patrol. What do ye and my daughter have between ye?"

Brin was taken aback, but not surprised. But how did one explain what they had? Especially after the issue during the storm. "Fair question, and I'll give ye an honest answer. I'm not sure."

Cailean arched his brow but his gaze stayed locked on Brin's. "Could ye elaborate on that a wee bit? I'm verra protective of the lass."

"As ye should be. She's a fine lass, verra talented. We've chatted a few times when she's been on patrol, probably the first time was on Cameron land. I like Ceit more than I suspected I would. I'm drawn to her warmth, her vivacity, her intelligence. We have interesting conversations, and she is a beautiful lass. I hope she is no' betrothed to anyone. Have ye arranged for her?"

"Nay, I have no'. She will choose her husband with Sorcha's and my approval. But she has no' expressed an interest in anyone yet. Do ye believe the interest is returned?"

Brin cleared his throat, thinking on exactly how to answer the man's question. Did Ceit care for him? "I do, but more importantly, I hope so. There is an age difference as I am over forty, but I dinnae see her that way. She's verra wise for her years, but she has shared something with me that may interfere with our brewing relationship."

A small smile crept across Cailean's face. "And that would be what?"

Brin let out a deep sigh, and he didn't care if the man caught his frustration. "She says she wishes to live on Ramsay land forever. And I'm sure ye know that I am heir to the chieftainship of Clan Cameron."

Cailean clasped his shoulder and said, "I see the truth of that statement. It would definitely be a problem."

"Yer thoughts?"

"My thoughts? 'Tis up to my daughter. She's the one ye must speak with about the matter."

"No advice for me? Would ye support our match if it came to it? Would ye give me her hand in marriage if I asked?"

The man chuckled. "That ye'll no' know until ye ask me."

Brin couldn't try to hide the defeat in his voice. He glanced over at Ceit and cocooned her hand inside his. "I look forward to Ceit awakening and becoming hale again. She's a mighty force on the battlefield, and a kinder person I've no' met."

Cailean's voice dropped to a lower tone, then said, "I'm pleased to see ye have feelings for the lass, and I believe ye would make a good husband for her. But would ye please tell me what happened in the cave?"

So stunned that he stumbled for words, he only managed to ask, "The cave?" Was he speaking of the two of them alone? How could he know?

"Word travels quickly among the clans. Surely ye know that much. Ye and Ceit were alone for one night when ye were separated from the rest of the patrol due to the avalanche. Exactly what happened in the cave?"

Cailean's eyes bore into his. This was Ceit's sire, so why was he so surprised? But he answered honestly. "I did no' compromise yer daughter, MacAdam. I have the utmost respect for her. We stayed inside, I built a fire, and true, she did sleep in my arms but solely for the purpose of giving her my heat. I didnae, wouldnae, violate yer daughter or any other lass. I hope ye would know that about my character as heir to the chief of Clan Cameron."

Cailean broke into a smile, then clasped his shoulder. "Forgive me for my inquisition, but a sire must test anyone who is interested in his daughter. Ye passed my tests, Cameron."

Brin did his best not to let Cailean see he'd been holding his breath, but as soon as the man left, he'd breathe a deep sigh of relief.

Cailean stepped around him and said, "I'm going to join my son before he eats all the food from the kitchens. But I'll tell ye this much."

Brin turned to look the man in the eye, hopeful it was something good.

"If both yer hearts will it to happen, ye'll find a way."

How Brin prayed that Ceit's heart would heal and will their relationship to continue. Gracie returned with a handful of linen strips and sat at her table. "I'll change her bandages the next time she awakens."

"Now that she has awakened, she'll be fine. Aye,

Gracie?" Brin had to hear the words from the healer.

Gracie set her tools down and looked up at him. "Ye know I canno' promise that, Brin. Surely, ye've seen enough patients on Cameron land who have lost much blood. 'Tis all about their inner strength, I believe. She has to wish to heal. And she must have the will to work at walking again. I'm sure she will."

Her answer sounded exactly like one his mother would give. She often spoke of people needing the will to live. He would do what he could to inspire her to live and not give up. He'd had pain from broken bones before. It was tough to get through at times. He could only imagine how hard it would be for Ceit to come back from her wounds and blood loss.

Gracie went back to her work, so he leaned in and whispered in Ceit's ear, "I love ye, Ceit MacAdam."

And what happened next surprised him. He felt good about that statement.

Indeed, he was in love with Ceit MacAdam. He had to wait to find out if she returned his love.

CHAPTER TWENTY-THREE

C EIT SAT IN a chair in front of the hearth in the great hall, a warm plaid covering her lap. Most had gone on to find their beds for the night, but she'd spent most of the day asleep. Because of that, she was no longer tired.

Brin came out of the kitchens carrying two goblets, one of ale and one of bone broth with a few vegetables mixed in. "Cook saved you a goblet of broth."

"Many thanks. It does make me feel better," she said, taking the proffered delicacy. At least it appeared to be a delicacy after their time in the cold and on patrol. "I love this broth."

When she'd awakened a couple of days ago, she'd had the odd memory of Brin confessing his love for her, yet he'd not said a word of it to her since then. But they'd often had others around. It pleased her, but she'd struggled ever since then as to what she would say if he said it to her now.

Did she love Brin?

If she ever loved a man, it would be Brin. The night they'd spent together was one of her favorite memories of all. But based on how badly she missed Ramsay land and her mother, sister, and grandparents, would she ever be able to leave Ramsay land?

"Ye are walking much better, Ceit. Do ye think ye'll be able to ride a horse? I'm happy to have ye ride with me if ye canno' ride alone." He moved a chair closer to her and took a seat, turning it slightly so he could face her.

She had considered that and had to admit she would prefer to ride with Brin over her father. "I would like to try on my own, but I know I'll no' be able to last, so I'll accept yer offer when I need it. My sire will have to accept it."

"Good. Ye are feeling better?"

"Aye. Much better, but I'm confused about something and I wish to ask ye a question." She didn't know how she was exactly going to go about admitting her weakness, but she was more than curious.

"Aye. I'll answer if I can." He leaned forward with his elbows on his knees, giving her his complete attention. She was grateful they were alone so she could speak freely.

"'Tis about the skirmish. I have no' had the chance to speak with Maitland or Thea or anyone else in the group. I was curious about a few things."

"Do ye have yer memory back about the battle? All of it?"

"I do. I recall hitting the one man in the chest and seeing him fall off his horse immediately. The man next to him was the one who hit me in the shoulder. His fury at my hitting his friend was more than evident. I was lucky to have knocked him off his horse with my next arrow, though 'twas no' a fatal injury. I struck him in his leg."

"'Tis hard to see a friend go down, especially if he dies. What else do ye recall?"

She glanced over her shoulder to see if anyone had entered the hall. Convinced they were alone, she confessed, "I recall striking the same man later, but then there were three men coming at me. But I was sweating and then I thought there were five in front of me. I couldn't see verra well so I shot into the middle of the group. I dinnae even know if I hit any of them. Could the first man have gone down and come back? Does that happen verra often? I'm wondering if my eyes played tricks on me. The number of men, the faces I saw, the injuries…" She knew she was rambling, but she had to settle this in her mind.

Then she did the one thing she swore she'd never do. Tears burst from her eyes and she was helpless to stop them.

"Ceit, why does that upset ye so? Because ye killed a man? It canno' be yer first. 'Tis part of battle. Ye had to know that when ye agreed to patrol."

Her head shook furiously because he didn't understand what upset her so. But she had to share her greatest fear with someone. Would Brin be interested in someone who was blind? "I dinnae know if I can continue to fight."

"Why? Ye dinnae have to, but after what I heard about yer battle, I'm confused by that statement.

Maitland said ye were amazing, that ye didnae back down, that ye had no fear."

Without consciously knowing it, she tipped her head back and wailed, "Because I couldnae see them." Her sob broke through and she set her goblet down and covered her face with her hands. "Am I going blind?"

Brin lifted her and settled her on his lap. "Ceit, ye were in battle." He pulled her hands away from her face and kissed away two tears. "Ye could have been sweating, could have had blood in yer face from another soldier. When most people fight, yer emotions take over, making everything different. Ye think differently, act differently. Yer body responds in odd ways, sending the blood racing though ye for one. Who knows what else is going on inside ye during battle? Or what else it could encourage ye to do. Do things ye may have never done if ye were on yer own. Why do ye say ye couldnae see them when yer accuracy was exactly correct? Maitland said ye scared the men. That doesnae happen from someone who is firing wildly."

She hitched a few times to try to control her sobs. At least enough to continue. She wished to hear Brin's opinion because he was older than she was. Her voice came out in a whisper. "But I dinnae know where I belong anymore. I think I'm losing my sight, Brin. What If I'm blind?"

"Blind? What makes ye say so? Ye canno' be blind if ye are hitting yer target."

"I fired wildly. I saw a blur and fired three

arrows. I was lucky. I dinnae see as good as I used to. I could be blind soon."

"Ceit, many older people lose their sight a bit. They dinnae go blind, but they just cannae see as far as they used to be able to see."

"But I'm no' old. And I canno' be an archer if I canno' see my targets," she wailed again. "What will I do with my life?"

"There are many things ye could do with yer life. What else do ye like to do besides shoot archery?"

"Naught. I've always focused on becoming the best. I wish to have the same reputation as my grandmother. She's known all over the land as the best archer of all. I'd hoped to gain that name for myself, but it canno' happen now."

"How is yer grandmother's sight?"

She scowled as he hit on one point she should have told him already. "She has lost a wee bit of her sight. When I worked with her before when we were on Ramsay land, she asked me if I was seeing the same, and I'm no'."

"So she has lost some of her sight, and she still has the same reputation?"

She frowned again but nodded her head. "But she didnae lose it until she was older."

"Did she tell ye that? Ye could be exactly like her. Ye have her accuracy and her gumption. Ye did no' back down in the height of the battle. That takes a special characteristic many dinnae have. But ye do."

"I dinnae know. I'm confused."

"So ye have no other interest if ye canno' be an archer?"

She thought for a moment. It was surely not weaving or planting a garden. She did enjoy working with Jennet when she'd been back on Black Isle. And she'd been fascinated watching Gracie.

"What?"

"I like learning about healing from Jennet. Ye were good with bandages, and I wish I knew more. I wish I could do some of the things Jennet was doing with the men who were hurt. She was so good with them, and I had the time to watch everything she did. Mayhap I should help our healers."

"'Tis a most admirable calling. Ye wouldnae have to travel to do so."

Ceit hung her head, swiping away at the last few tears she had, glad she'd finally been able to control herself. She rarely cried, but when she did, it was not pretty. "I'll think on it. Talk with my mama. Mayhap she has an idea of what I can do with my life besides go on patrol. I dinnae think I have many more days to do so."

Brin set his fingers under her chin and lifted her gaze to his. "Mayhap ye belong with me." He kissed her, at first tenderly, but then an all-consuming kiss that left her breathless.

Perhaps he was right.

They left Grant land and stopped at Cameron land to rest before continuing on to Ramsay land because Ceit was so anxious to get home. She had tired easily so the group agreed to let her rest before moving on. The poor lass was so exhausted that she went straight to bed once they arrived, his mother gladly assisting her and checking her wounds before she slept.

Brin made his way out to the stable later that night. They'd be leaving in a day or two for Ramsay land and he'd agreed to go along. Any time before they planned a journey, he liked to check on their horses, make sure he chose the right mounts for their trip.

He was surprised to hear a noise at the gates, something that rarely happened at this hour. Most should be in their beds, not out in the forests where animals and reivers lay in wait. He heard the sobs of a woman and turned to find out who was there.

Stepping outside the gates with two Cameron guards, he was surprised to find Uncle Ruari there with a woman, nearly unrecognizable. Her sobs slowed once he stepped outside, but her hair was in disarray, and he barely recognized her.

Abigall MacKie nearly fell off her horse and crumpled to her knees in front of him. "Brin, Brin. Please help me. I hate him. I love ye. It has always been ye. He…"

Stunned by this sudden admission, he needed the entire story, so he forced himself to use his best reasoning skills. "Abigall. Are ye hurt anywhere? Do ye need a healer?"

"Nay. I had the bairn and he…"

"Please come inside and explain everything to me," he said, steadying her but she froze and stared at him with a look he would have enjoyed many years ago.

No longer. The oddest sensation happened to him, something he'd not experienced in years. He looked at Abigall, his long-lost love, and had no feelings for her.

None.

Ceit was the only woman for him.

"Brin, I wish to marry ye. Can ye no' end my marriage to Odgar? I hate him. I never loved him like I did ye. Please take me back. If ye accept me back to my old clan, he'll have to leave me be." Abigall rambled on and on, her tremors telling him more than her words.

He guided her inside the curtain wall, across the courtyard and into the keep, glancing across the hall and pleased to see his mother coming out of her healing chamber. "Mama, Abigall needs yer help."

"Nay, I need ye, Brin." The woman swung around and clung to his tunic, trying her best to tug him closer, but he set her apart from him.

Her mother came up behind them, placing her hands on the girl's shoulders. "Abigall, tell me exactly what happened," his mother said as she guided the distraught woman over to a chair in the healing chamber. His father entered behind Brin, casting a perplexed face his way. Brin shrugged but took a seat on the other side of the table away from Abigall. His mother sat next to the woman.

"I had our bairn. Odgar said he wished for a son and when the bairn was born, it was a wee lass. He took her away from the midwife and wouldn't allow me to see her until later. Then he slapped me and said the next one better be a son or he'd beat me." Her tears erupted and her body shook from the stress she was under. "He was so angry that I feared for my life. What shall I do? I canno' stay married to a man who will beat me."

His mother did her best to tame Abigall's wild hair, setting some of it to rights, but then said, "Aedan, please find a lass to assist me. I must check to see that Abigall has healed properly. Brin, please talk to her. Abigall, Brin canno' marry ye, just so ye have no expectations."

"But why no'? We were meant to be. Always and forever."

His father left to find some help for his mother, something Brin was grateful for because he did not wish to assist with this examination.

"Because ye are married to a chieftain and that canno' be undone. Ye have bairns with the man."

"But Brin…"

Brin moved over and took Abigall's hands in his and said as kindly as he could, "Abigall, I love another. We canno' be. I expect to be betrothed in a short time." He struggled inside because he wished to beat the bastard for hitting a helpless woman, especially one who'd just delivered a bairn. He wasn't exactly sure how to handle this situation since Odgar was a chieftain. This was something he needed to discuss with his sire.

Fresh tears rolled down her cheeks at this

revelation, something that must have taken her by surprise. "Ye love another?"

"Aye," he said quietly. "Abigall, we were together a long time ago. We were both young. I think ye need to speak with yer husband once ye have healed."

A lass came in and said, "My lady, may I be of assistance?"

Brin wished to use this as a good time to take his leave. "I'll be on patrol, Abigall, so I will say good-bye to ye."

Abigall swiped at her tears and said, "I understand. I guess I dinnae truly love ye either. I just wish to escape my husband."

His mother said, "Aedan will help ye with that. If ye wish to come back to Clan Cameron, ye are welcome. Yer parents are still in the village. Once the morrow is upon us, I'll have them brought to ye. And ye can go back for yer new daughter, if ye like."

"Many thanks to ye, my lady. Brin, I wish ye happiness."

He nodded and took his leave before something else came up. He was about to run up the stairs to his bedchamber when his sire came into the great hall. "Brin, we need ye at the gates. MacKie is here."

He cursed under his breath but then followed his sire out the door and through the courtyard. Once they neared the gates, he could hear Odgar raising his voice. He sounded as though he was deep in his cups.

Brin stepped outside the gates, his sire directly

behind him. "Odgar, yer wife is here and my mother is tending her. She needs care."

"Send her out or I'll knock yer gate down myself."

Brin whistled, something he'd trained his men to listen for in case an emergent situation ever came upon him. Instantly, ten guards showed up bearing various weaponry.

"Nay, ye'll leave the gates alone. Ye are in yer cups. I suggest ye go home and come back after ye've had a good sleep," Brin said, crossing his arms. He wasn't going to allow the man to bully him. Apparently, he spent most of his life bullying people.

"I want my wife. The bitch defied me. I told her to give me another son and she gave me another bitch. I'll show her."

"Ye are naught more than a big bully, MacKie. If women could control whether they bore a lad or a lass, we'd only have lads. They canno' so stop trying to make her pay for it. 'Tis no' her fault."

"And I suppose she asked to marry ye. Asked ye to get her away from me so she could marry ye."

Aedan glanced up at his son, a small grin on his face.

"It wouldnae matter if she did ask me. I love another and I expect to be married within a year, so take yer leave. I'm not interested in marrying yer wife, but I am interested in keeping her from an abusive husband."

"I'll treat her as I like." The man swayed on his horse and the beast pranced in response.

His father said, "Ye will go back to yer land,

MacKie. When ye are sober, ye can return and speak with her parents. 'Tis up to them what happens next. Up to Abigall and her parents. I'll have my men escort ye home."

The man tipped to the side and fell off his horse, falling into a deep sleep instantly. Brin said to two men, "Put him on his mount and take the reins. Take him home and leave him inside his gates."

Then he stepped back inside the gates to his own courtyard. His sire followed him, clasping his shoulder. "Ye've made yer decision?"

"I have. We'll see if she accepts me. Please say naught at this point. I must court her as she deserves."

"Understood. Am I correct that ye feel a wee bit free right now?"

Brin smiled at his father. "I do. I have no feelings for Abigall at all. My feelings are for someone who deserves to be loved with my whole heart. Someone who is strong, smart, and beautiful. I've found her, Da."

Finally.

CHAPTER TWENTY-FOUR

THE PATROL GROUP left Cameron land two days later, Cailean, Cadyn, and Ceit, along with five guards assigned to travel with them to Ramsay land. It had been an easier ride than the last few they'd had—no snow and no battles.

Abigall's parents had come for her and brought her to their home. He had no idea what else had transpired, but his sire had said he would tend to the issue. For that he was grateful. He wished to focus on Ceit, not a woman from his past.

Ceit had been quiet but strong, not giving in to her weakness at all. Brin had watched her ride alone, her head high, but he could almost tell when it became too much for her. She'd slowed her horse and looked at him, shaking her head.

He moved his mount closer and lifted her off her horse, settling her in front of him. "Take a nap, lass. 'Twill make the trip go faster."

She did exactly that and he liked her where she was, though he was aware of her father and brother's constant looks their way. But nevertheless, he was glad to be on Ramsay land where he would not be under their watchful gazes all day.

Then what was he to do? He'd set Ceit on a task to uncover her purpose, but he still wasn't certain of his own. Protecting Cameron Castle didn't seem like something that would keep him busy enough to please himself. He preferred to be productive and moving.

They made it to Ramsay land just before dark the following day, so he helped Ceit down and she went straight into her mother's arms once they were inside the courtyard.

Torrian came along beside him. "And just like that, she disappears. Her family is here and they've all been worried about her. Allow her mother and grandmother a day or two to fuss over her, then things will be back to usual. Ye had an interesting patrol, I hear."

"Aye," Brin replied, deciding he'd enjoy speaking with Torrian for a bit. "The English we've encountered are not part of any cavalry. Instead they seem to be random reivers brought up from the Borderlands."

"So the patrol has gone after the ones who escaped?"

"Aye, I will join them in a day or two. I wish to see that Ceit has made it home safely. She had a tough situation. Two wounds and someone had to pull the tip of the arrow out. Thea did a fine job."

"So I have heard. The group was here for a short time, then moved on." Torrian took a step closer to lower his voice. "I detect a more serious interest in Ceit MacAdam than patrol peer. Am I correct?"

"Aye, I'd like to marry her someday, but please tell no one. I must see how she feels. She's had much to deal with so we have no' discussed it."

"Ye will make a fine couple."

"Will I be able to get her away from Clan Ramsay once in a while? Ye know I'm to be chieftain of Clan Cameron, though even that thought concerns me."

Torrian tossed him an apple from a barrel and pointed to two tree stumps outside the stable. "Sit. I'd like to hear more. What concerns do ye have?"

Not ready to argue with the chieftain, he took the proffered treat and sat down, taking a bite to give him time to settle his thoughts. "Are ye ever bored as chieftain? I've spent most of my time training our guards. To do naught every day sounds boring."

Torrian arched a brow at him. "Naught? My duties are about tenfold, so I dinnae think of them as naught."

Brin stared at him. "Tenfold?" He'd never thought there were that many things to tend.

"Aye. I oversee care of all the cottages inside the wall and out. Ordering repairs when needed. Kyle and I tend to all disagreements. We sit as judges for all complaints within the village. Thefts, those types of things. I am in charge of making sure we have enough food for all. If our harvest is low, I must buy grain from other places. With my wife, we discuss the wool we have and what we may need to supplement in order to clothe everyone. And as ye know, 'tis the chieftain who decides weaponry with the armorer, handles the fleet of horses. And…"

Brin held his hand up. "I understand. I hadn't thought of it that way, but I can see it takes more attention than I thought."

"Dinnae forget the ale supply ye must keep going to make everyone happy. Hunting, wine, boots, and leather. They all come to ye for their needs. Ye'll see soon enough. Do ye no' ever follow yer sire around for a fortnight or so?"

"I guess I have no'. I will do so when I return home."

"Ye should. Ye could be taking on yer duties anytime soon. My sire just decided one day that it was time for me to take over. Then Gavin took over training of swordsmen and Gregor the archers. Yer sire is advancing in age, as ye know."

Brin knew Torrian was right. He'd ignored all the possible duties he'd have as chieftain. It was time to face them. Take over some of the duties from his sire once patrol was finished.

"Now all I have to do is convince Ceit that Cameron land would be a good place to live."

Torrian shrugged. "Put her in charge of yer archers. That will surely keep her busy. Ye've always needed more."

Now that was a great thought.

Ceit sat in her bedchamber trying to decide what to do next. Coming home to see her mother had been wonderful, but she hadn't talked with either of her grandparents yet.

She was afraid to.

Word had probably reached them about how she'd been unable to see how many men were attacking her at the end of the skirmish. She still didn't know. Had she seen three or five? Her mind continued to play tricks on her, casting doubts at every turn.

She pushed herself up, readying herself to go into the great hall when she stopped abruptly. Her beloved grandmother stood in the doorway, her arms crossed, staring at her. With her wisdom and her tendency to speak the truth, she had a feeling her grandmother was here to tell her she knew all about her failings as an archer.

Why had she been born to the daughter of Gwyneth Ramsay, the woman known as the finest archer in all the land? The archer who had the reputation of being able to strike a man in his bollocks, having pinned a man to a tree once who had dared to steal her daughter and niece away and hide them. She'd left him there, the arrow perfectly placed in his groin, the man bleeding out for all to see, while she'd rescued Brigid and Jennet from a box buried in the ground.

Every man who looked at him covered their private parts with their hands.

"Greetings, Grandmama."

She dropped her gaze as she sat back down in the chair, landing with a plop.

"Why are ye no' looking at me, lass?"

Dammit all to hell, but why was the woman so astute?

"I'll look at ye. I was just arranging myself. My arm and my leg still pain me some and I dinnae wish to tear out my stitches. Ye know how Aunt Brenna gets about them." Rubbing her leg, she brought her gaze up to her grandmother's even though she feared she could look to her insides from just one glance.

Her grandmother sat down on the bed opposite her. "I heard all about yer battle. I thought I would come and hear it from ye."

There was no sense in lying anymore about her failings. In fact, she was going to be brutally honest about them. She got out of her chair and sat down next to her grandmother, bursting into tears as soon as her bottom hit the bed. Her grandmother opened her arms and she fell into them, sobbing against her. "I'm sorry, Grandmama. I always wished to make ye proud of me. I canno' see right anymore. I'll never be able to go on patrol again. What will I do with my life now?"

The woman let her sob a bit before setting her back to look at her. "What are ye talking about? I heard ye scared half the Englishmen away. Said ye shot into a group of three men and hit them all. They ran scared. In fact, Maitland said he heard one of them mumbling about Ramsay women archers. I'm proud of ye, lass."

"They said that? Maitland didnae tell ye? Or Brin?" She swiped at her tears, trying her best to ebb the wild flow.

"Tell me what?"

"That I couldnae tell if they were three men or five. They'll never allow me on another patrol."

"Ceit, those things happen in battle. And besides, ye probably have the same eye problem I have. I couldnae see half of what I fired at."

Incredulous at that statement, she sat back and stared at the woman. Was she being honest? "'Struth?"

Her grandmother nodded. "Do ye know how I kept my reputation?"

She shook her head.

"Yer grandsire told me where to shoot half the time. Once I passed twenty years, my vision slowly worsened. He'd look at where I was aiming and then tell me to move a wee bit to the left or the right. But I can still see, just like ye can. We can see shapes and sizes. 'Tis no reason to quit."

"It isnae?" So shocked by the conversation, her tears finally stopped, only a hitching left.

"Nay, ye'll no' be quitting. Ye take that last tale and stretch it as far as ye can. Yer grandfather and yer father will tell anyone who listens how ye sent the English running away. The Scots love those kind of stories."

"So how did ye manage to be so accurate when ye were after the villains? Especially the ones who were after Brigid and Jennet?"

The dear woman in front of her snorted then chuckled. "I'll tell ye a secret if ye promise no' to tell anyone."

"I promise."

"I was aiming for Bearchun's throat when he kidnapped my lassies. It was sheer accident that

I hit him in the bollocks, but I didnae care. It stopped him, and the men all talked of it. Over and over and over again."

She began to giggle and her grandmother laughed with her. "I love ye, Grandmama."

"I love ye and I'm proud of ye. Now dinnae dare tell yer grandsire what I said. And remember this. Ye are one of the finest archers in all the land. Ye sent the Englishmen running because of what ye did. Believe in yerself."

"And ye can still see well enough?"

"I see well enough to have taught ye and all yer cousins how to shoot, did I no'?"

"Aye. Will ye be upset if I marry someone and leave Ramsay land?" She hated to blurt the truth out but she had to mention the possibility.

"Ye are in love with the son of one of our finest allies. I'd be thrilled to see ye as the mistress of Clan Cameron. Ye'll come back often."

The two headed down to the great hall, both smiling. Grandpapa stopped them and said, "What did ye two speak of?"

"Naught ye need to know about, Logan," her grandmother said. Then she winked at Ceit just as Brin came up on her other side. "Take good care of her, Cameron. I'm watching ye."

Brin glanced at her, unsure of what to say to her grandmother. So Ceit leaned over and whispered. "I love ye. 'Tis all ye need to know for now."

"I love ye too," he whispered.

CHAPTER TWENTY-FIVE

B RIN SAT ACROSS the table from Ceit, her smile lighting up the hall. It was just after the midday meal and the group at the table had been reliving the last battle when Ceit had fiercely taken on several Englishmen, even while wounded.

He was glad to see her smile and her laughter was as sweet as any sound he'd ever heard. The door to the great hall opened and a messenger entered with Kyle Maule. Maule called out, "Brin Cameron, the message is for ye."

Brin got up and headed toward the door, the group now abuzz with curiosity, but no one more curious than he was. He prayed it wasn't bad news about his parents.

"What is it?" he asked Kyle, Chief Torrian suddenly appearing at Brin's side.

The messenger said, "Clan Cameron is under attack by the English. Yer sire is requesting yer help along with a score Ramsay guards if ye can spare them, Chief." The messenger looked from Brin to Torrian.

Brin couldn't even speak, the shock causing his

mind to go absolutely blank. Ceit came up beside him, her arm snaking around his waist. "What happened?"

"Clan Cameron is being attacked by the English. I have to go," Brin said, nearly heading to the door but Torrian stopped him.

"Brin," Torrian said. "Ye'll wait a quarter hour for a force to go with ye. I will join ye, but we will go as an organized group, not haphazardly. If we dinnae, we will be asking for more trouble. Meet me at the stable in a quarter hour and we will leave. Kyle, choose yer men. I'd like at least two score. One will guard the abbey and the other will go to Cameron Castle. Divide them with that consideration. And also send three men to Grant land immediately to request their assistance. We'll take whatever help we can get."

Logan appeared behind Torrian. "Who the hell is attacking Aedan Cameron? Are they daft? No one attacks the abbey."

The messenger said, "They are English."

"A cavalry in uniform?" Torrian asked.

"Nay. English by their words."

"Are they attacking the abbey also?" Brin asked.

"Nay."

"How many?" Kyle asked.

"Mayhap three score. And some have wounds. Bloody breeches in tatters," the messenger explained. "They've been battling elsewhere and won."

"Anything else we should know?" Torrian asked.

"Nay. 'Tis all I know, Chief."

"Logan, take him to the kitchens so he can fill his belly, then gather Gwyneth. I'd like her input." Torrian headed out the door.

Kyle bellowed, "All guards be at the stable within five minutes."

The hall became a cacophony of chair and stool legs hitting stone as various guards gathered their wives in a hug and headed out the door. They all attended the midday meal so it was not uncommon for so many to be inside.

They were not there long.

Brin rubbed his chin as thoughts bounced around in his mind. Logan took the messenger to the kitchens, then found Gwyneth and the two headed toward them.

Ceit said, "I'm going with ye."

"Nay, ye'll no'." Brin couldn't believe she would even consider such a thing. "Ye are no' fit for battle yet, Ceit. Ye'll be hurt worse. I could no' fight worrying about ye also. I have to find my sire. He's no' so great with a sword with his advanced age."

Logan called out from their approaching place. "Ye are no' going, Ceit MacAdam. I can see yer plan in yer shoulders, but ye havenae fully healed yet."

Gwyneth shook her head at her beloved granddaughter, her arm wrapping around her shoulders when she came upon them. "Ye'll slow the group, Ceit. Brin, Maitland's group is no' far away. Logan and I can ride for them. They are farther south, but ye could use their help."

Logan added, "Gwynie, with yer hip bothering ye so, ye need no' go. Stay here and I'll go."

Gwyneth glared at Logan and said, "Ye think ye can stop me, old man? I dinnae think ye can. My hips are fine on horseback."

Brin had a sudden understanding of where Ceit's stubborn streak came from—her grandmother. At her advanced age, she did what she wished to do. He had to admire her.

Logan grinned and said, "Fine, join me then. We may no' have to travel far, as my guess is they have already heard and are headed back here for an update. They could be there fighting already." Then he kissed his wife's cheek and said, "I still love yer fiery spunk, Gwynie." Then he bellowed, "MacAdam, ye need to watch her." He pointed to Ceit who glared at her grandsire.

Brin heard Ceit groan at that declaration, not surprised to see her sire headed toward her, but he needed to go and not worry about her. If she were hale, it would be different. He'd welcome her help. The lass had an eye like a hawk after its prey, even if she didnae believe it.

Cailean came up behind his daughter. "I'll tie her up if I must, Brin. Go ahead and do what ye must. I'll see that she stays here."

Ceit glared at her sire. "I could help. I could assist his mother bandaging the injured. I've learned some, if ye must know."

Brin leaned over and kissed her on the lips, not caring what the others were to say. "And I would welcome that help. Why no' have yer sire bring ye along in two days? The battle should be done by then. But for now, I must go. My thanks to ye, Cailean. I would worry about yer daughter. She's become verra important to me."

He left. He had to. His parents. His father… his mother…Uncle Ruari…Aunt Julia…their bairns. So many to worry about. Who the hell would attack Cameron land and the abbey?

Logan and Gwyneth followed him out to the stable. Once outside the keep, the old geezer's voice caught him just right. "Think ye the chieftainship of Clan Cameron is important enough now for ye? And what about the abbey? Protecting God's property is no' important either?"

Brin could not deny any of his words. "Ye are right and I was wrong. Now will ye do what ye can to help me? And if no' me, then my sire and my mother? We would greatly appreciate any help ye can give us. Ye can chastise me all ye want after this is over."

"I will do whatever I can. Ye have my word on that."

"Can ye tell me why they are attacking my clan? No one ever attacks my clan. I dinnae understand it. I've no' seen anything like it." Brin was so upset he couldn't comprehend exactly what was happening. Why. By whom. What their goal was. He had to know all these things about the enemy before you could plan your attack. He could not strategize blindly.

Torrian said, "Keep walking and we'll explain along the way."

They arrived at the stable while Kyle gave his orders to all the men, Lily hugging him in between his orders of who rode in which group. Torrian joined them and said, "They attack yer land and the abbey for the same reason as always, Brin. The treasure. Word always travels about treasures in abbeys. And Lochluin has one of the largest treasures, but I'm sure ye are aware of it."

He sighed. "I am, but I thought it was a forgotten fact."

"Never. Be prepared for the group to plan on taking over yer castle, then storming the abbey. I'm sending three score, and I'm sending word to Connor Grant. If we can add the patrol group to our numbers, we'll be in great shape."

"Many thanks to ye."

"Torrian, Gwynie and I are going in search of Maitland's patrol. We'll send them yer way. I suspect they are less than a few hours south of here. 'Tis possible they could be not far from Edinburgh."

"We'd appreciate it, Uncle Logan. Brin, ye'll ride with me behind Kyle's front line, explain anything ye think could help about yer land, any hiding spots to be aware of. Reyna and Wulf will ride with us. I wish to have Wulf look at the English, see if he recognizes the group. Guide us through yer landmarks. I think we know most of what we need to know about yer land, but things change every winter."

"Understood. Yer help is gratefully appreciated. And Logan?"

"Aye?"

"I'll be a mighty proud chieftain of Clan Cameron if the castle still stands."

Logan leaned back and clasped his shoulder. "It takes some men longer than others to learn their purpose. I think ye are about to learn yers, Brin Cameron. Fight with wisdom and cunning, not with yer emotions. Dinnae be foolish and we'll rid the land of the English bastards."

He prayed Logan was right.

CHAPTER TWENTY-SIX

CEIT STOOD ON the parapets with her
father, watching the wave of Ramsay guards
leave their land, their columns so impressive in
their blue plaids going across the meadow and
down the hill that it brought tears to her eyes.

"Cadyn will be fine, Da."

"I know he will. And so will Reyna and Wulf.
He's good to have around, see if he recognizes the
English group at all."

"How long do ye think they'll be gone?"

"Four or five days probably."

"Truly that long?"

"I dinnae know for certes but get the idea out
of yer head. Ye'll no' be sneaking away. I already
warned the stable lads about ye stealing a horse."

Good thing she'd already counted on her father
doing exactly that, so she hid a horse in the forest
anyway. Though she would wait a few hours to
go.

She was not much of a traveler at night.

"Da, if ye must know, I still tire easily. I think I
will take a wee nap if ye dinnae mind."

He set his arms across her shoulders. "Do yer wounds still pain ye?"

"Aye, a wee bit. But they are much better. Ye know how it can be." She recalled all the stories of her sire in battle—how tough he was, what a talented swordsman he was. But her favorite story is the one when he had gone over the side of a ravine just to save her mother. And her grandfather had been there to yell at him too.

"I do, though I have little memory of the worst injury."

"Da, do ye really no' recall when ye hurt yerself going over the ravine long ago?"

Her father chuckled, his eyes lighting up at the memory of the journey they took to Grant land, the famous time when her grandfather had finally agreed to Cailean and Sorcha's betrothal. He'd jumped off a cliff to save her mother. "The only thing I recall was red mud caked all over me. My legs, my arms, even my head."

"Red mud? 'Tis no such thing, is there?"

"Nay, 'twas my blood mixed with the mud. I had that many bruises and cuts on me. It's still the only time yer grandsire admits to worrying about me. Said I wouldn't let go of yer mother and that I'd lost half my mind because of the pain I was in." He paused and stared over the parapets. "Which wound bothers ye more?"

"My shoulder is fine. The wound in my leg hurts more. I'll no' be running any races in the Ramsay festival this year."

"There'll be many more, lass. Heal yerself first. Go ahead with yer nap. I'll go find yer mother."

They headed down the stairs to the second level, though it was slow going for her on the stairs. But each day she improved. Once she stepped inside her chamber, she sat down, the guilt of defying her parents washing over her.

Yet her determination to help Brin was stronger. They'd forgive her. They had to understand that she couldn't sit here with some foolish needlework in her lap while she worried about Brin and Clan Cameron.

She had to help him. How would she feel if Ramsay Castle were under attack? She couldn't fathom such a travesty. In her present state, she was perfectly capable of climbing a small tree and shooting her arrows from the perimeter of the battle.

Vowing not to do anything foolish, she just had to go find him. Make sure he wasn't hurt. Make sure his parents were fine.

She loved Brin Cameron.

Brin passed Lochluin Abbey, Kyle sending one group of guards to do battle there. "Gavin, ye are in charge of the swordsmen. Gregor, handle the archers."

The group split while the remaining guards followed Brin to Clan Cameron. Brin's gut dropped the closer he came to his land, especially when he could see the dust from battle, the cries of pain echoing across the landscape.

He said a quick prayer to find his parents hale. His gaze scanned the area close to the abbey, looking for any identification as to what group they were. Why the hell were they here? Brin asked Wulf, "Know ye any of these men? Where they are from?"

Wulf said, "Nay. They look to be little more than a large band of reivers. The kind who fight closest to the Borderlands. In fact, I'd wager a good many of them are here to fight for the coin. They are no' strong swordsmen and I dinnae see many archers. We'll send them scurrying south, do no' worry yerself."

Torrian said, "Brin, ye fight where ye must. Look for yer sire or yer uncle. I'll handle the men."

Brin spurred his horse forward, circling the melee for any sign of his father while Torrian gave orders to his guardsmen. He saw Uncle Ruari and others he recognized, and they were beating the English easily. But they were also outnumbered, something that didn't sit well with him.

His uncle yelled to him, "He's at the rear of the melee. Near the curtain wall."

Brin found a narrow path toward the curtain wall and headed in that direction when he was set upon by four Englishmen. He had little trouble taking them down but whenever one fell, another replaced him. He swung his sword with ease, doing his best to focus but also taking a moment here and there to look for his sire.

He finally found him a good distance away but not far from the main gate, the one closed and unbreached by the bastards yet. There were a few archers atop the wall, shooting anyone who tried to throw a rope up to climb the wall and come inside.

Brin had to protect his mother, her small frame standing in one corner watching over the battle zone, a pile of rocks stacked in front of her. Her resilience amazed him. If she had to, she would strike one in the head with a rock. She would know where to strike best.

He guided his mount off to the edge so he could monitor the side of the curtain wall, pleased to see there were no warriors there yet. Then his gaze caught his sire again. All of a sudden, a large group surrounded his sire.

"Take the chieftain down!" one bastard bellowed, others joining him in the foray quickly. Brin found himself possessed with a fury he'd not felt before.

Fury and fear.

"Da! Watch yer back!"

There were several Cameron guards nearby doing their best to protect their chieftain, but they were becoming outnumbered. "Fight, Da!"

Brin cut down two men in front of him, moving a wee bit closer, but then the worst happened. An English bastard caught his sire's left arm, his blade striking hard and then bouncing off to catch the edge of his father's leg at the same time.

"Kill the chieftain!"

Brin nearly vomited as he watched his father fight, blood now pouring out of his two wounds. He had to get closer to him so he swung his sword with a ferocity he didn't know he possessed, striking one, then another.

"Uncle Ruari! Da! Protect him!"

His uncle spun around and moved his horse back to protect his brother, but then he was struck over his shoulder arm, losing his sword.

Out of nowhere came a slew of arrows, firing in rapid succession from behind him. The three men directly in front of him fell so he moved closer to his father. Uncle Ruari was in front of his father now though he had no weapon, his sire now weaving on his horse.

He was going to fall to the ground. He'd be trampled by the huge warhorses around him.

"Da! Hang on!"

"Brin! Get yer sire before he topples off his horse!"

It sounded like Ceit. Two arrows hit the chest of the men in front of him, clearing the way, so he took a second to look into the trees at the edge of his property.

Ceit was in one tree while Merewen and Reyna shot from the tree next to him. "Ceit, stay there. Dinnae dare move from that spot!" he bellowed.

If she would stay there, he could tend his sire. His father glanced over at him and shook his head. Brin roared, "Get the hell off Cameron land!" He swung at two near him, taking the sword arm from one and knocking the second off his horse. Two arrows sluiced not far from him, taking out two more.

"The chief is going down! Cameron Castle will be ours!" one fool shouted.

His father struggled to stay on, but he was about to lose his mount.

CHAPTER TWENTY-SEVEN

B RIN BELLOWED THE Cameron war whoop and headed straight for his father, striking with a madness that possessed him. His father tipped one way but Uncle Ruari pushed him back up, then everything around him disappeared as he watched his father fall from his horse.

The Cameron chief hit the ground hard.

His mother's scream rent the air from the parapets.

"I am the Cameron chieftain, not Aedan Cameron. I am his son and I am the chieftain. Ye have no' won yet!" His voice carried across the sea of English warriors, a sudden onset of Grant plaids joining them.

Arrows flew overhead. Connor Grant's war whoop called out to all the English who had a sudden change of heart when they saw the size and number of the Highlanders and their warhorses flood the area. He noticed Alasdair on another monstrous warhorse, showing off in the middle of the group by going up on his hind legs while Alasdair bellowed the Grant war whoop, scaring off many.

Brin couldn't have been more pleased to see Connor and Alasdair Grant and their men. He fought off the ones around him. "Grant!" he called out to Connor. "I need to get to my sire. He's on the ground."

Connor caught on, made a sign to Alasdair, then led the group away from his father, drawing them and killing with a precision he hadn't seen in a long time. He made it to his sire and jumped off his horse. He knelt down and lifted him gingerly. "I have ye, Da."

"Son, ye are the new chieftain. I may no' make it." Brin took a ripped piece of his sire's tunic and tied it above the cut on his arm to slow the blood pouring out of him.

His father's blood stained his clothing, but his eyes were still as alert as ever. "I accept it, Da, but ye are no' leaving us yet. I need yer help. Ye must fight. I wish ye to be here when I marry Ceit MacAdam."

His father nodded and closed his eyes with a small smile.

Arrows continued to hit men around him while the Grant warriors cut the English down easily. Cries of pain and grunts of men and beasts made it hard to hear his father, but he laid him across his horse and mounted, guiding his horse toward the gates.

Connor yelled, "Go through. We'll keep the bastards back."

A sudden sea of red and green plaids surrounded

them, opening up a direct route to the gates. The wooden doors opened and he made it through, his uncle behind him. His mother's voice carried to him. "Brin, ride to the doors and we'll get him inside the healing chamber."

He did as his mother suggested as she barked orders out to the older men who had stayed inside the gates. "Open the doors!"

They managed to get him inside, Brin carrying him over to the healing chamber and setting him down gently on one of the beds. His father looked so small in the bed, something he found odd because his father had always seemed larger than life itself.

"Da. Ye need to fight." He helped loosen some of his clothing so his mother could assess his wounds.

"Are they winning?" he managed, a weak smile. "After all these years, we're finally going to lose. I had no idea they were coming."

His mother appeared next to him. "Save yer strength, Aedan. Listen to yer son. We are no' going to lose. Connor Grant just arrived with his warhorses. Did ye no' see all the red plaids next to the blue ones and the brown ones?" She removed her husband's tunic and covered him with a dry plaid so she could study his wound. "Ye are no' going to die, Aedan. But ye've lost a bit of blood. Start drinking. Ye know my rule."

His mother fussed around the chamber while Brin held a goblet of ale for his father to drink. "Connor will win, Da. His warriors made a path for me straight to the gate. Dinnae worry."

The door to the healing chamber opened and Ceit hurried in, no hesitation at all from her wounds. "How is he?"

Brin reached her quickly, drawing her in for a quick hug. "Why are ye here? Does yer sire know? Yer grandsire?"

"Nay. I snuck out, but dinnae worry about me. I'm hale. The Grants took care of the rest of the English. Alasdair is tying up the ones who are still alive. He plans to question them about the attack."

His father said, "Is this the lass who is to be my daughter-in-law? I believe 'tis Ceit, but my vision is blurry."

Brin pulled her over and said, "Aye, this is Ceit. She was firing arrows from the trees like a woman possessed." He kissed her forehead then wrapped an arm around her shoulders. "Da, keep the rest to yerself."

"Why?"

Ceit drawled, "Because he has no' asked me yet." She gave Brin an elbow to his side.

His mother said, "I'm pleased by this topic, but I'm worried about our clanmates. And what about the abbey? Are they done fighting there? Someone told me there are two different battles going on."

Ceit said, "I'll find out for ye."

"I'll go," Brin said.

"Nay, ye stay with yer da," Ceit said, pulling away from him.

His father said, "Stay, please."

He stepped back and sat on a stool next to his

sire and said, "I'll stay. Ceit, let me know as soon as ye find out all that is transpiring around here."

"I will." She blew him a kiss and left.

Brin had a sudden urge to keep her from going anywhere. But his sire distracted him completely.

"Brin, I thought I'd died out there. I started to see my life pass in front of my eyes." He stared over Brin's shoulder in a daze.

"Ye are no' going to die, Da." Thinking on his father's words, he decided to pursue it a wee bit more. "What exactly did ye see that makes ye say so, Da?"

His father rubbed his eyes, then said, "I swear I saw Alexander Grant on his horse Midnight, Brin. Am I going daft?"

Brin said, "Nay, Papa. 'Twas Alasdair. He looks exactly like his grandfather." Then he stared after Ceit.

"Hurry back!"

CHAPTER TWENTY-EIGHT

CEIT STRODE BACK outside, giving in to her desire to favor her leg with the wound. She hadn't hurt it much, but it did ache a bit more. Sitting in a tree didn't help, but she'd made it, and Brin had survived.

She prayed his sire would come through.

After all, she heard there was to be a wedding. Hers! Her wedding to Brin. That thought did indeed make her smile. She'd assess the situation here and at the abbey, then she would return to help Jennie with the wounded.

Perhaps that would become her purpose. Helping Brin's mother and learn healing from her. Outside the gate, Connor Grant was busy assigning his men to different duties. To her surprise, he was talking with her brother Cadyn. Connor waved her over, asking for an update. "Uncle Aedan? Will he make it?"

"I think so. He lost quite a bit of blood, but Jennie thinks he'll be fine. He'll be hurting as he has two injuries, but Brin is here to help. Cadyn, ye are hale? No injuries? I know Da was worried."

Cadyn said, "I'm fine, sister. I doubt Da will be pleased to find out ye are here too." He grinned and said to Connor. "She snuck out. She was supposed to stay behind."

Connor held both palms up and said, "I'm staying out of this one. 'Tis yer clan, no' mine. Ceit, glad ye are hale."

"I am fine so my sire will be fine too, Connor."

"Good. Where are ye headed?" Connor asked.

"I'm going to see what is happening at the abbey."

"I'll send a few men with ye as ye should no' be traveling alone yet. There are still many stragglers."

"Stragglers?"

"Men who ran once they saw the English were losing the battle. They may no' have a horse and might want yers. Travel with care."

"I'll gladly accept yer escort. Cadyn, are ye staying here?"

Her brother said, "I'm headed out to meet Maitland. They're on their way here."

She waved to the two men, then mounted her horse, traveling between the Grant guards as they headed across the meadow toward the abbey. The sound of battle had dissipated, so she hoped it had ended. Once they were close enough to see the abbey, to notice that there was no one battling in front, she waved to the men, "I need to make a stop."

They nodded, and she led them over to a copse of oak trees, the kind of bushes that gave good cover. She hadn't noticed how badly she had to relieve herself until the bouncing had begun on her horse. She'd be quick about it so she could head over to the abbey.

Once she finished, she headed back toward her horse when a voice caught her—one that she didn't recognize. She turned around to see if someone was behind her, but she saw nothing. That made her hurry back to the Grant men. She was just about to break through the copse to Connor's men when someone grabbed her by the hair from behind.

She tried to scream, but instead, her world went black.

Brin glanced around the chamber, then moved over to the door to open it and peer out into the hall.

"What is it, Brin?" his mother asked.

"Ceit said she would return with news, but she's been gone too long. I was checking to see if she was held up in the hall chatting with someone."

"Go find her. Ye know 'tis chaos out there, even if the Grants are in control. The English run away and then steal."

He nodded, glancing over at his sire, but his mother said, "Aedan will be fine. He just needs to eat and rest. Go!"

He did as she suggested, heading out through the courtyard and into the area surrounding the castle, full of a mix of red plaids and blue plaids among the Cameron plaids. He found Connor and asked, "Have ye seen Ceit about?"

"Aye. She said she was heading to the abbey so

I sent three of my men with her." Connor looked over his shoulder, easy to do because he was so tall. "Those three men. Shite." He strode around Brin and spoke to his men. "Where is she?"

"We lost her," one said, gasping for his breath. "She stopped to take care of her needs and never returned. Unfortunately, we let too much time pass before we searched for her. Whoever stole her away was fast and quiet. Or mayhap there was more than one. They moved with stealth. We never heard a thing and searched the area thoroughly. We decided to return to make ye aware of the problem before we continued our search."

"She was on foot or horseback?" Brin asked.

"On foot. We left her horse in case she returned. It also marks where she disappeared."

Brin's insides caved in as if he just didn't know how much more he could bear. Bad news was in full force this day. He ran his hand down his face, forcing himself to focus on what news was important. The abbey. "Is there battle still going on at the abbey?"

"Nay, 'twas quiet. Many wandering around, Ramsay guards controlling the area. I didnae see anyone else where we stopped. 'Tis why it surprised us that she disappeared."

Connor said, "We'll help ye find her." He gave instructions to another man, then motioned for Brin to mount up and the group headed out. "We'll find her, Cameron."

He prayed they would.

CHAPTER TWENTY-NINE

CEIT AWAKENED IN a quiet clearing, her hands bound behind her next to a tree she was seated near. It wasn't the best position considering her shoulder, but it had healed enough not to make her scream in pain.

A group of six men stood a short distance away, none dressed in plaid but instead in various dark clothing, stains of blood evident on some. She didn't recognize the area they were in so they had to be a distance from Cameron land. They spoke quietly, and one turned his head noticing she was now awake.

Should she have feigned sleep?

Ceit took a deep breath, willing her insides to calm down because she knew she'd be rescued. They were in a world full of Ramsay, Cameron, and Grant warriors who'd be looking for her and would find her. Time. That was all she needed—time.

She'd keep the men talking and someone would rescue her.

One of the men spun around and stalked over to her, his gaze locked on her as an evil grin crossed his face. He stopped in front of her, his arms crossed, his legs in a wide stance.

He looked vaguely familiar.

"There you are, you evil witch. It's time to pay for your sins, my sweet. Your fine looks will not get you anywhere with me or my brother."

Another man joined him, chuckling. "Can I take her first, Edwin?

"Nay. She is mine to do with as I wish."

"Who are ye?" she asked, willing herself to calm and think of as many questions as she could. She had to keep them busy, the dagger in his hand telling her to be very thoughtful about this process. He seemed to want her specifically, not just any lass.

The man called Edwin knelt in front of her, a wicked grin on his face. "Do you not recognize me? I'm the one who put that wound in your shoulder, hardly a fair price for killing my brother."

His brother? Who was his brother? She racked her brain as the fool talked on. He was the one who wounded her…

The skirmish. The one with the English with Maitland and Dyna after they left Black Isle. She'd hit a man in his chest and he'd fallen off his horse just before the man next to him had fired and struck her in the shoulder.

This was the man. This was why he looked vaguely familiar. "Ye did this to me?"

"Aye. And now I choose to finish you, but fair is fair. I had to watch my brother die after you hit him in the chest and he fell off his horse. After the battle, I managed to get him on my horse and leave the area. I was sure I could save him but you hit him in the worst spot. After we rode a bit, his belly ripped open and his intestines spilled out almost into my hands. He looked up at me and begged me to help him... his last words. He died begging me."

She couldn't think of any response.

"I lost my dear brother because of *you*." The finger pointed directly at her, a hiss coming out between his teeth as if he were a snake ready to bite.

She argued, "'Twas a battle ye started. If ye had stayed in England where ye belonged, naught would have happened. 'Tis yer fault yer brother died, not mine."

"Silence!" The man called Edwin roared. "Your fault, not mine. You struck him with your arrow, not me. You will pay for it." He tipped his head backward to the other men. "An eye for an eye the Bible says."

Three men hurried behind the tree, then returned with another man between them. One who was kicking furiously, his hands and feet bound, a gag in his mouth.

Cadyn.

She gasped, unable to hide it.

"You recognize your brother, aye? Good. I'm glad to see he does mean something to you. Some hate their own siblings, but not you. I need it to be so, or this would not work."

"What are ye talking about?"

"Do you not understand?" He tilted his head and grinned, bending at the knee, his face covered with a look of glee that told her he was daft. He pointed back to her brother.

She began to understand what was going to happen, an odd sickness pooling deep in her belly.

"You killed my brother in front of me, I will kill yours in front of you. I'll put him right on your lap after I stab him and allow his guts to spill out all over...YOU!" The last word came out in such a loud shout that she started, her arms scraping across the tree. Then he spun around and walked over to Cadyn.

Then the oddest thing happened. A soft finger trailed across her hand, and she knew it was Brin. The tree was a large oak in the middle of a forest, leaves and debris everywhere. He must have found a way over and was hiding behind the tree. Probably lying flat so as not to be seen. There were two trees next to this one to help hide him.

Cadyn struggled against the men, making loud noises enough to draw everyone's attention to him. In the chaos, a voice whispered around the tree. "Dinnae worry. I will set ye free once he turns away, but ye canno' move until I tell ye. More are coming before I can do so."

She touched his hand to let him know she understood, but now her eyes fixed on her dear brother. His eyes were wild and furious at the same time. She stared at him, willing him to calm down.

Out of the farthest edge of the clearing came the shriek of a woman. Covered in leaves and dirt, an old woman squealed in pain, her hands covering her eyes as she stumbled toward her.

Her hair was in disarray and she was dressed like a man, limping terribly. "My eyes! I'm blinded! What happened? Someone help me. I can no longer see anything. Help me, please!"

"Grandmama?" Hellfire, as quickly as she said it, she regretted it. But had she truly lost her sight or was this some game she was playing?

How she prayed it was false.

"Ceit? Is that ye? Speak again so I can find ye." She clutched something against her chest as she cautiously stepped forward, measuring each step carefully.

"Nay, go back, Grandmama. Leave us."

"Where are ye? I must find ye." Her dear grandmother moved forward, coming directly toward her, a shawl in her hands. She tripped and landed in Ceit's lap, dropping her shawl next to her.

Edwin yelled, "Get her."

Two men grabbed each arm of her grandmother and lifted her up, tugging her back away from Ceit. With all the attention on her, Brin cut Ceit's bindings. It took all her strength not to reach out for her grandmother, but she did as Brin had instructed. She kept her hands together as if they were still bound. If her grandmother was here, so was her grandfather. They'd concocted something. She just needed to be patient.

"Why, this is absolutely perfect. Now I have another of your beloved relatives who I can kill in front of you. First your brother, then this old witch, then I'll finally kill you. Slowly." The daft man paced back and forth in the middle of the clearing, his gaze darting around.

Ceit glanced at the shawl her grandmother had dropped next to her, now lying in an odd configuration, but then she knew why. Her grandmother had left a bow underneath it, hidden by the shawl. If she were to wager, she would guess there were a couple of arrows there too.

That gave her hope. Brin had cut her bindings and she could grab her bow as soon as he told her to do so.

A man stepped into the clearing behind where her grandmother had entered. He carried a large sword and strode into the middle of the group, moving close to Edwin's brother.

Grandsire!

The group of six men stood stunned. It took three to hold Cadyn now, one other held onto her grandmother along with Edwin's brother, and Edwin stood not far from Grandda. She did her best to stifle her grin because she had a good idea what was coming.

"In case ye fools dinnae know who ye hold captive, allow me to explain. My name is Logan Ramsay. Ye are holding my granddaughter and grandson hostage, and the other old witch ye have right there? That would be my wife, Gwyneth Ramsay. Have ye no' heard of her before? Because ye should pay attention to who ye take captive."

Two men visibly stepped away from Gwyneth, shrinking, clearly aware of her reputation. One mumbled, "Gwyneth…"

A second finished his words, "Ramsay? This old woman?"

"She's blind, you fools, so she cannot hurt you," Edwin shouted. "Ignore the old man."

Her grandfather continued his rant. "And nay, she isnae blind, but she is too close to shoot ye in the bollocks. But..."

Edwin dropped to his knees and grabbed Ceit by the hair. "Do anything and I'll slice her neck in front of you. I want her blood on my hands. Stand back, all of you."

"Suits me just fine," Grandsire bragged. "Ye think ye'll hurt my granddaughter before ye find an arrow between yer eyes? Or mayhap between yer bollocks. Gives Gwynie a better distance to aim, and she has help with her. If ye look hard enough, ye might see that archer in the trees and that one over there, and the one over there... She's my beloved grandniece." He turned and pointed to one spot covered with leaves and to another and to another, but none of the archers were visible to the men.

"They are all expert archers. Ye'll see."

"I'll kill her right now!" Edwin declared, sweating profusely, pulling Ceit closer. But then he moved his hand with the weapon and swiped at the sweat on his forehead.

Grandda scratched his head, his famous signal, and three arrows flew out of the trees, catching three of the men. Ceit brought her head back hard, away from his dagger, hitting her captor in the forehead, causing him to drop his weapon. Edwin turned and ran.

Brin came out from behind the tree and chased after him. "Defend yerself, Edwin, or I'll drop ye right now." Edwin spun around revealing a small sword and Brin swung out, catching his leg, the bastard falling to his knees but then managing to stand again. He let out a blood-curdling bellow and lunged for Brin, but Brin was faster, plunging his sword into Edwin's belly just as the English fool was hit with two arrows in the chest.

His brother turned tail and ran. "I'll leave this one to ye, love." Brin turned around as Ceit grabbed her bow and arrow, shooting the brother in the back, dropping him to the ground with a scream of pain.

Two more arrows came out of the trees, and once the six men were either dead or unable to fight back, Wenna, Dyna, and Thea dropped onto the ground.

Maitland strode into the clearing and clasped Grandda's shoulder. "Well done, Logan. Still, old man, ye know how to give us more tales to tell. I was a wee bit nervous when he had his dagger at Ceit's throat, but ye knew him best."

Her grandsire shouted, "Cadyn, ye are hale?"

"Aye, Grandda. Many thanks to ye." His hand rubbed at his neck as he approached them. "Daft bastards."

Her grandfather shook his head and said, "Daft Englishmen. They have no brains. Can barely get their heads out of the clouds."

Brin helped Ceit up and she threw her arms around his neck.

"Ye are hale, lass?"

"Aye, I'm no' hurt. But I promise ye, I'm never going on patrol again."

CHAPTER THIRTY

BRIN TOOK CEIT'S hand and led her away from the clearing where she'd been held captive. He was surprised to see they were not far from the abbey, and he had a compelling need to step inside to thank God for an end to their peril.

As if reading his mind, she said, "I'd like to go too. No more patrols for me."

"Truly? You mean it?" He squeezed her hand as they made their way to the abbey.

"No' the way I feel at the moment. Two injuries and a kidnapping. Nearly freezing to death in a storm. What more could happen? I think I need to read the signs and step back for a bit. And ye?"

He sighed. "I once thought that being Chieftain of Cameron Castle was no challenge. I've been challenged enough. I want things back the way they were. No more English fools on our land. No more snowstorms…" Then he gazed into Ceit's eyes, seeing just a flash of hurt there. "Forgive me. The storm was actually one of the best things that ever happened to me."

She tipped her head in confusion. "What do ye mean?"

"Ye. We would no' be us if no' for the snowstorm. We would have passed each other in the storm and continued. In fact, ye are my challenge, Ceit MacAdam. Come with me. I owe a prayer of thanks to God before I do anything else."

He led her to the abbey and inside, the nun at the front desk waving to him. "I need to visit the chapel for a moment, Sister." All the nuns knew him, so the woman nodded and went back to her work.

They made their way down the passageway and into the chapel. Humbled by its beauty, he stopped for a moment at the back of the church, looking at the altar, the cross, the simple carved wood.

"Logan was right. It is more than enough for me to protect the abbey as the new chieftain of Cameron Castle. I accepted it from my sire. He'll no' be able to perform his duties for a while. Mayhap 'tis time to allow him to rest." He swiped at a tear that fell down his face, then moved into a pew and knelt to say a few prayers of thanks.

When he finished, he squeezed Ceit's hand. "When I saw ye tied to that tree, then the dagger at yer neck, I never felt such fear. I'd just watched my sire struck down from his horse, bleeding profusely, and heard my mother scream. Thought my world was about to end—first with my sire, then with ye. I canno' wait any longer."

"What are ye saying, Brin?"

"I'm saying I love ye, Ceit. That I want ye by

my side forever, to be my wife as we accept the humble duty of protecting Cameron Castle and Lochluin Abbey. Will ye marry me?"

"Aye, Brin. Naught would please me more."

He cupped her face and kissed her, a passionate kiss of possession, of promises for their future, of sweet beginnings. His tongue dueled with hers and he was pleased to find her as wanting as he was. When he ended the kiss, he leaned his forehead against hers and whispered, "What say ye about marrying now. Right now. I'll find a priest or the abbess, either can marry us. I'll just have to get my sire and mother here, then we could marry. I see no reason to wait. I'm too old to wait!" He grinned at his last declaration.

"But my parents…"

"Ceit!"

Her grandsire's voice carried down the passageway.

"Must he yell everywhere he goes?" she whispered to Brin.

They stepped out of the chapel and she asked, "What is it, Grandsire?"

"Yer mother is here looking for ye. Yer father is talking with Cadyn so I said I'd search for ye. She needs to set eyes on ye, lass, so come out to the front of the abbey. She's seated on the bench under the trees."

Ceit said, "Wonderful. I'll be right there." Then she turned to Brin and uttered one word. "Now."

Her grandfather turned to leave, but Brin called out to him. "Logan, please wait a moment."

He turned back around and waited.

Brin approached him, his hand still entwined with Ceit's. "I have asked yer granddaughter to marry me and she has accepted. I love her with all my heart, and I have also accepted the chieftainship from my sire. I would like yer approval, if ye would. I will ask Cailean next. And yer daughter, of course."

He kissed Ceit's cheek, who had a broad smile on her face.

Logan crossed his arms and narrowed his gaze, first at her, then back to him. "So ye have accepted yer purpose? Ye've decided that protecting Lochluin Abbey and Cameron land is a worthy purpose?"

"Aye and nay."

"Explain yerself."

"Protecting the abbey and our land is indeed a worthy purpose, and I do accept it. But 'tis no' my primary purpose."

Logan arched a brow at him.

"Loving Ceit and making her happy is my purpose."

"Och, ye've finally figured it out. Took ye a long time to discover yer primary purpose."

"Like yers is for Grandmama," Ceit said.

Her grandfather smiled. "Gwynie is one of my main purposes, but no' my primary purpose. I'll let ye think on it a wee bit before I tell ye."

"I'm sure Ceit can figure it out," Brin said, glancing at her.

"I have no idea."

"Truly?" Brin asked, staring at her.

She shrugged. "None."

Logan laughed, spun on his boot heel and left. "Go find yer mother, Ceit, before she attacks me."

CHAPTER THIRTY-ONE

THEY MARRIED THE next day, his mother insisting on making sure that his father would be hale for the day. After the wedding, the group gathered in the courtyard in front of Cameron Castle.

Ceit thought it a wondrous time to marry because there were so many of their extended family in attendance.

The entire patrol was there—Alaric, Tevis, Maitland, Willum, Wenna, Thea, Reyna, and Dyna.

Connor Grant and his soldiers—among them Alasdair, Alick MacNicol, and Drostan.

Many Ramsays—her grandparents, her parents, Gavin and Merewen, Gregor, and Torrian.

And of course all the Camerons who were grateful to have their clan and homes still standing and thrilled with their new chieftain. They danced and feasted grandly on pheasant, venison, lamb, and as many meat pies as the kitchen could prepare on short notice.

But her fondest memory was near the end of

the night when the youngest of the group settled around the hearth chatting.

Brin looked at the group and said, "We're so pleased to have ye all. And so grateful for all who came to assist us. Many thanks to ye all. But I do have one question. Connor, how did ye get here so quickly? We'd just sent the messenger to ye."

Alasdair chuckled. "Because I'd just traveled from MacLintock land, and I saw a group that I knew would be trouble. I only traveled with five, so we didn't approach but we went to the next town and discovered they were headed to Cameron land. As soon as I told Connor, he had his warriors ready to travel."

"Ye can always count on Clan Grant to send a slew of warriors," Torrian said. "So ye are the new chieftain of Cameron Castle, Brin? I think ye'll do a fine job."

Brin said, "Papa likes to tell me 'tis my purpose in life, but I think my purpose is to make Ceit happy." Ceit sat next to him and he had his arm around her shoulders while she leaned into him.

Cadyn said, "Ye'd be wise to do so. Ye have me, my sire, and my grandsire to answer to."

That brought a line of oooh's from the crowd.

Brin drawled, "I hadn't considered that yet."

Gavin asked, "How could ye no' have thought of that? Ye had to at least considered Grandsire would be watching."

Her grandsire marched in and took a seat near the hearth, then snorted at the comment. "He couldn't have thought of it, or he'd never have married ye, Ceit. I feared ye'd never find one who would dare take on the three of us. And aye, MacAdam, I'll admit ye are a force to be dealt with, especially when it comes to yer women."

"Had I considered, I would have stilled married ye, Ceit. I think ye are my destiny, my purpose."

"Is that what purpose means?" Alaric asked. "I've heard others talk about it, but I was unsure of its meaning."

Dyna said, "'Tis what the heavens wish ye to do. Ye could have more than one purpose, but one is always more important than others."

Brin leaned over to give his wife a kiss on the cheek. "Ceit is my first purpose, the clan second, but equally important." Ceit snuggled against him, her seat so close they were touching.

Gavin said, "Brin, ye belong as chieftain. 'Tis yer purpose, what ye were meant to do, just like Torrian's purpose is to be chieftain of Clan Ramsay."

Maitland said, "Tad says the same is his purpose." Tad was his eldest brother already in place as chieftain of Clan Menzie.

Torrian added, "I think my wife is my purpose, chieftain is second."

Alasdair said, "I have the most unusual purpose then."

"What do ye think yers is?" Connor asked. "Mine is Sela. I was chieftain second. Then my bairns and grandbairns. Do ye no' think Emmalin is yer purpose?"

Alasdair said, "Nay. Emmalin is such a strong woman that she doesnae need me. My purpose was to protect Grandsire."

Ceit looked over at her grandfather, a wide grin on his face. The old man crossed his arms and declared, "Alex needed one. I dinnae."

Dyna was apparently not impressed with Alasdair's announcement, glaring at him. "I was Grandsire's protector. No' ye, Alasdair. Derric and I found him in the cottage."

"But I was always watching over him."

Maitland said, "Some people deserve two protectors. We'll agree to both of ye."

Torrian looked at his uncle and said, "When did ye first realize yer purpose? When ye first met Aunt Gwyneth?"

Her grandfather grinned. "As I told Brin and Ceit, Gwynie is one of my purposes, but not my primary."

"Then what?" Torrian asked.

"Ye mean who?"

"Alright. Who?"

"Who, Grandsire? I have no idea," Ceit said. "Do ye, Cadyn? Mama?"

Her mother shouted, "Me! I'm his purpose."

Logan snorted, "Sorcha, ye dinnae need any protection with MacAdam around. The man jumped over a cliff for ye, lass."

Her mother leaned over and gave her father a kiss. "Then I dinnae know either, Da. Do ye, Gavin?"

Gavin shook his head.

Torrian got a smug look on his face. "I know."

"Who?" A dozen voices chimed in to stare at Torrian.

"Brenna."

Logan got a small smile on his face, leaned back in his chair, and said, "The day I stole Brenna Grant from her home, I became her protector. I stole her right from under Alex Grant's nose, though he says he knew it and followed me, but I dinnae believe him. Right from the start, there was something about her that called out to the heavens."

He teared up, leaning back to balance his chair on the two back legs. "When I brought that woman through the forests, something happened that I still canno' explain. The path cleared so much that I knew something was up. 'Twas as if the faeries had made a path for me. We'd just left the trail on the way north and it was overgrown and wild. Though there were branches, it was nearly as though the path was lit up for us in the middle of the night. We traveled in half the time it took us to get to Grant land.

"The closer we got to my brother, the more the clouds disappeared. Understand that Quade was lying near death in an abandoned cabin, his two bairns were near death on Ramsay land. But when I brought her into that cabin, and dawn broke, the sun was out stronger than I'd ever seen it.

"One of my guards said it was eerie because it was so bright. When was the sun ever that bright in the middle of a forest? I had to agree with him. I didnae argue with her because she had a gift I didnae comprehend. I still dinnae. She saved the man when I was sure he would be dead by the time I got back. Brenna Grant is the closest thing to an angel I've ever met. I love ye all, but there's something different about her." He stopped because his words caught in his throat. "And she is the piece that united the Grant and Ramsay clans."

When he was able to continue, his voice came out in a soft whisper. "Brenna brought happiness to my brother, saved Torrian's life and Lily's, and brought our clan back together. She's given me nieces and nephews, grand nieces and nephews whom I adore, and healed more people I love than I can count. Gwynie was my second purpose, but Brenna Grant was my first."

"I miss my sire," Torrian said.

"I do too, your sire and my own," Connor said.

Ceit said, "I wish Uncle Quade was here with us."

Brin added, "And Uncle Alex."

Dyna pursed her lips and said, "I was no' saddened when Grandpapa left us. He was ready. The oldest person I've ever met. And with the sharpest mind. He was ready to see Grandmama."

Grandda sighed, "It saddened me when Quade left us, but after living with all the pain he had for so many years, it was time. And that last fall he took was verra hard on him. He never recovered from it fully. He was pleased to see his bairns grown and happy, and Brenna had all the grandbairns to fuss over. He told me the day before he passed that he was ready. I couldnae fault him. And his last words I'll always remember."

Torrian looked at him and arched his brow. "Well? Ye must share now. He's my sire."

"He said, 'I die a happy man, brother. My thanks to ye for the greatest favor ye ever did for me. Bringing Brenna to me.'"

No one said anything for a while, but then Maitland said, "What a tale, Logan. My thanks for sharing."

"What is yer purpose, Maitland?"

Maitland rubbed his hands together and said, "I dinnae have one."

Her grandfather moved over to stand in front of Maitland and said, "Menzie, I dinnae have seer talents much like others in my clan, but I see this much. Yer purpose is coming soon."

Grandsire climbed the staircase to his chamber but stopped at the top of the balcony. He turned around and said, "Maitland, there is another woman who needs ye. Ye'll see soon enough."

Every face turned to look at Maitland and they all witnessed the same thing.

Tears rolling down his face.

EPILOGUE

About a month later

BRIN AND CEIT lay together, arms intertwined, on the bed in his parents' old cottage in a hidden part of their property behind the castle. It was the middle of the night and the section of the thatched roof was pulled back so they could both see the stars because it was a clear night.

Brin's hand slipped across her abdomen again, back toward her breasts, his skilled fingers knowing exactly where to touch her, his caress sending waves of desire coursing through her body.

"When ye touch me like this, I can barely keep still, Brin Cameron."

"I know. 'Tis quite a tease, but the slow caress makes ye so slick that I can enter ye with one quick thrust," he said, his voice so husky that it traveled straight to her core.

Neither had any clothing on, the cool night teasing them alternately with the flames of the fire in the hearth on the wall opposite the bed.

"I also love when I can see yer excitement as much as I feel my own." Her eyes traveled to his traitorous member, standing as majestically tall as it had ever been. She waggled her brow at him but said nothing, her tongue licking her lower lip, something she knew made him daft with need. Sometimes he hated the power he'd given her, but usually he loved it.

He stilled because he knew exactly what that look of hers meant, his eyes catching hers in the light of the moon. He watched as she crawled onto her hands and knees, moving over him to take him by mouth. One long lick with her tongue brought out a groan of lust that he couldn't contain. Then she took him in her mouth as deeply and slowly as she could, running her tongue back up his length before she lifted her mouth to play with him, pulsating against his most tender spots with that tongue of hers.

In between her taunts, he watched her smile. "Ye enjoy this, ye wee minx."

"I surely do, my chieftain."

He narrowed his gaze and she moved over him until he took one nipple in his mouth, grazing his teeth across the sensitive tip. She cried out, that little eek that always drove him wild.

With one swift move, he got up, tossed her onto her back and held himself over her, up on his elbows. "Ye are quite a tease, Ceit Cameron. I can stand no more of yer taunting ways."

"Then finish this," she said, arching her back up before she grabbed the dark hairs on his chest, tugging him down.

She spread her legs and he entered her with one thrust, her slick entrance welcoming him. He buried himself deep inside, moaning with the sheer pleasure of finding himself home, that favorite place of his unlike any other. He stilled himself for fear of losing his seed too quickly. That wouldn't do at all. He had to bring her to completion first because he loved watching her, even in the moonlight.

More in the moonlight. When he was back in control, he pulled out and plunged back inside her, still holding his weight on his elbows. He did this three times, her eyes opening and closing with each movement. And that quick moan.

"Faster," she begged.

"My pleasure," he whispered, his breath coming out against her ear and she shivered with need, just the way he liked.

They hit their rhythm together as they rocked in the bed, continuing until he hit her just right. He knew by the pattern of her breathing, that little gasp growing to a feverish pitch. When she hit the note he waited for, he reached down between them and touched her in just the right spot, and she screamed his name as she climaxed, arching against him. Her sounds drove him over the edge and they finished, nearly together, but not quite.

He always preferred her to go first.

He fell back onto the bed, grasping her hand and squeezing. "I swear it just gets better and better."

"I agree. I had no idea it could be like this." She

swallowed, doing her best to slow her breathing. "And to think I thought I would never marry. What a fool I was."

"And to think I thought I would never fall in love. I was the bigger fool."

———∾∾———

Ceit sat in the healing chamber with Jennie, learning how to mix potions. Jennie said, "Ceit, ye are a fine student. I've never seen anyone learn as quickly as ye have."

"Because I enjoy it. I never knew that I had the heart of a healer, but I believe I do." She'd worked with Jennie often since coming to Cameron land, and she'd learned something new every day. It pleased her because she could see how Brin's mother had aged, that her hands couldn't open the containers as easily, or that she moved slowly whenever she had to work in one position for a long time.

"I dinnae say this lightly, but I am compelled. I'd wished to say it before, but I forced myself to wait at least a month. Now I can speak my thoughts. I am so happy ye and Brin found each other. I've never seen him so happy and it gives this old mother joy to see it."

"I adore yer son, Jennie."

"I see it in yer heart every day, lass. Ye need no' tell me." She patted her hand lovingly.

The door opened and Brin's voice called out to them. "Ceit, are ye here?"

He stuck his head in the healing chamber and said, "A package has arrived and 'tis for ye."

She said, "Truly? For me? Who would send me something?"

He took her hand and said, "Come into the great hall. 'Tis on the table near the hearth."

She followed him into the hall, not surprised to see his sire seated near the hearth. He'd healed, though slowly, but now he had an odd grin on his face. Jennie came along behind them.

Jennie looked at his sire and gasped, "Aedan Cameron, I have seen that look before. What have ye done now?"

Aedan said, "Jennie, sit down. I had little to do with it. Ye'll see."

She took a seat near the fire while Ceit looked up at Brin. "What is this about?" She glanced about the hall, noticing they were the only ones inside. Brin must have sent the others out.

"Remember I told ye that sometime I would find the perfect wedding gift for ye? Well, I have and it finally arrived."

Ceit gave him a puzzled look but touched the package gingerly.

"Open it."

The package looked to be about the size of a pair of boots, so she wondered if that was what sat inside, but she said nothing. Her curiosity was more than piqued, so she untied the twine, and took the outer wrapping off, finding a box inside.

"Boots?"

"Nay."

"Should I shake it and guess?" she asked.

"Nay. Do no' shake it. Ye could break something."

More curious than ever, she continued, lifting

the top of the box off carefully. She peered inside and had no idea what it was.

There were four different sets of glassware encased in wires, but they were all quite odd looking. "What is this? Glassware of some kind? For what?"

He lifted out one set and rearranged it a wee bit, then set it against her face, placing the two pieces of wire over her ears. She pulled on them and tried to move them. "I canno' see what ye are doing, Brin. They're in the way." She tried to move the glassware away from her face but he stilled her hands.

"Look, Ceit. Look through the glass parts. They are supposed to help ye see better."

She stepped back and took her hands away while Brin dropped his. "Look over there at the tapestry on the far wall."

She gasped, then broke into giggles. "I can see it! I havenae been able to see that far in a long time. 'Tis so beautiful."

His mother said, "Ye know about this, Aedan. I can tell." His father grinned.

"Come with me," Brin said, taking her hand and opening the door so they could go outside.

She followed, giggling and gasping at every new thing she could see. "Look at the leaves still left on that tree. It's so pretty. They are all red and gold. And the pine tree. I can see the needles. And I can see everything. Everything. Where did ye find these?"

She took them off and stared at them. "Brin. Where? How?"

The monks told me about a man in Italy who was making these for people. They call them eyeglasses. I thought they could help ye."

"But there are more in the box."

"One for yer grandmother. And they are all a wee bit different. Different strengths. Ye'll have to try them on to see which one works best for ye."

She hugged him, holding the glasses in her hands, tears running down her cheek. "Brin, I love ye so much. Thank ye."

They moved back inside so she could try on the other glasses.

Her mother said, "Brin, what a wonderful gift. Even better than paper."

Aedan asked, "Better than yer book?" He'd given her a special book of anatomy as a wedding present."

"Och, nay. I'll have to show it to ye someday, Ceit."

"Do I look funny with them on, Brin?"

"Nay, I vow you've never looked more beautiful."

www.keiramontclair.com

NOVELS BY KEIRA MONTCLAIR

HIGHLAND HUNTERS
THE SCOT'S CONFLICT
THE SCOT'S TRAITOR
THE SCOT'S PROTECTOR
THE SCOT'S VOW

HIGHLAND HEALERS
THE CURSE OF BLACK ISLE
THE WITCH OF BLACK ISLE
THE SCOURGE OF BLACK ISLE
THE GHOSTS OF BLACK ISLE
THE GIFT OF BLACK ISLE

THE CLAN GRANT SERIES
#1- RESCUED BY A HIGHLANDER-
Alex and Maddie
#2- HEALING A HIGHLANDER'S HEART-
Brenna and Quade
#3- LOVE LETTERS FROM LARGS-
Brodie and Celestina
#4-JOURNEY TO THE HIGHLANDS-
Robbie and Caralyn
#5-HIGHLAND SPARKS-
Logan and Gwyneth
#6-MY DESPERATE HIGHLANDER-
Micheil and Diana

HIGHLAND SWORDS
THE SCOT'S BETRAYAL
THE SCOT'S SPY
THE SCOT'S PURSUIT
THE SCOT'S QUEST
THE SCOT'S DECEPTION
THE SCOT'S ANGEL

THE SOULMATE CHRONICLES TRILOGY
#1 TRUSTING A HIGHLANDER
#2 TRUSTING A SCOT
#3 TRUSTING A CHIEFTAIN

STAND-ALONE BOOKS
ESCAPE TO THE HIGHLANDS
THE BANISHED HIGHLANDER
REFORMING THE DUKE-REGENCY
WOLF AND THE WILD SCOTS
FALLING FOR THE CHIEFTAIN-3RD in a
collaborative trilogy
HIGHLAND SECRETS -3rd in a collaborative
trilogy

THE SUMMERHILL SERIES-CONTEMPORARY ROMANCE
#1-ONE SUMMERHILL DAY
#2-A FRESH START FOR TWO
#3-THREE REASONS TO LOVE

DEAR READER,

Thank you for reading Brin and Ceit's story. My favorite stories to write are always those that unite two from our clans. It allows me to bring up tons of their history—about Brenna, Torrian, Quade, Aedan's gift to Jennie, Padraig and Giselle, even bringing Alasdair into the story.

So much so that the next story will be Maitland's and Maeve's story, another about two from our beloved clans, though neither are known as well as Brin and Ceit.

Aedan's gift of paper for Jennie (in The Brightest Star in the Highlands) had such a reputation that Brin wished to do the same for Ceit. What better present than the gift of sight?

As always, I play with history a wee bit. The first mention of eyeglasses was back in the 10th century, and it's almost always tied with one church or another. Why? Because most people could not read back then, only the monks and those who learned so they could read the Bible. It was the monks' job to transcribe scriptures and laws, so they also needed glasses.

In the 13th century, credit is mostly given to one or more Italians for making eyeglasses of convex glass that were made to be worn. So sending a messenger to Italy was not a stretch for the chieftain of Clan Cameron. Messengers often traveled between abbeys.

See you at Maitland and Maeve's Christmas story!

Keira

ABOUT THE AUTHOR

KEIRA MONTCLAIR IS the pen name of an author who lives in South Carolina with her husband. She loves to write fast-paced, emotional romance, especially with children as secondary characters.

When she's not writing, she loves to spend time with her grandchildren. She's worked as a high school math teacher, a registered nurse, and an office manager. She loves ballet, mathematics, puzzles, learning anything new, and creating new characters for her readers to fall in love with.

She writes historical romantic suspense. Her best-selling series is a family saga that follows two medieval Scottish clans through four generations and now numbers over forty books.

Contact her through her website:
www.keiramontclair.com.

www.ingramcontent.com/pod-product-compliance
Lightning Source LLC
Chambersburg PA
CBHW070913180626
46817CB00003B/1037